SHE WANTED LOVE

"Do you really think that I would want to marry a man who is old enough to be my grandfather? The answer is quite simply *'no'*."

Cyril Warner sat back in his chair.

"Are you really so stupid, Eleta, as to think that is your final word?"

"Of course it's my final word. Have him on your Board, which I am sure is a very wise move, but I have no intention of marrying an old man and certainly not one who is marrying me for my money!"

There was silence for a moment and then he said,

"You have forgotten one thing."

"What can that be?" Eleta asked suspiciously

"That I am your Guardian by Law," her stepfather replied, "and you have to obey me until you are twenty-one. That, as I ascertained this morning, does not happen for nine months and by then you will be on my instructions married to the Duke of Hazelware."

Eleta stared at him.

"Do you really intend to force me up the aisle with someone I have no wish to marry, an old man who is marrying me for what I possess and not for myself?"

THE BARBARA CARTLAND PINK COLLECTION

Titles in this series

SHE WANTED LOVE

BARBARA CARTLAND

Barbaracartland.com Ltd

THE BARBARA CARTLAND PINK COLLECTION

Dame Barbara Cartland is still regarded as the most prolific bestselling author in the history of the world.

In her lifetime she was frequently in the Guinness Book of Records for writing more books than any other living author.

Her most amazing literary feat was to double her output from 10 books a year to over 20 books a year when she was 77 to meet the huge demand.

She went on writing continuously at this rate for 20 years and wrote her very last book at the age of 97, thus completing an incredible 400 books between the ages of 77 and 97.

Her publishers finally could not keep up with this phenomenal output, so at her death in 2000 she left behind an amazing 160 unpublished manuscripts, something that no other author has ever achieved.

Barbara's son, Ian McCorquodale, together with his daughter Iona, felt that it was their sacred duty to publish all these titles for Barbara's millions of admirers all over the world who so love her wonderful romances.

So in 2004 they started publishing the 160 brand new Barbara Cartlands as *The Barbara Cartland Pink Collection*, as Barbara's favourite colour was always pink – and yet more pink!

The Barbara Cartland Pink Collection is published monthly exclusively by Barbaracartland.com and the books are numbered in sequence from 1 to 160.

Enjoy receiving a brand new Barbara Cartland book each month by taking out an annual subscription to the Pink Collection, or purchase the books individually.

The Pink Collection is available from the Barbara Cartland website www.barbaracartland.com via mail order and through all good bookshops.

In addition Ian and Iona are proud to announce that The Barbara Cartland Pink Collection is now available in ebook format as from Valentine's Day 2011.

For more information, please contact us at:

Barbaracartland.com Ltd.
Camfield Place
Hatfield
Hertfordshire AL9 6JE
United Kingdom

Telephone: +44 (0)1707 642629
Fax: +44 (0)1707 663041
Email: info@barbaracartland.com

THE LATE DAME BARBARA CARTLAND

Barbara Cartland who sadly died in May 2000 at the age of nearly 99 was the world's most famous romantic novelist who wrote 723 books in her lifetime with worldwide sales of over 1 billion copies and her books were translated into 36 different languages.

As well as romantic novels, she wrote historical biographies, 6 autobiographies, theatrical plays, books of advice on life, love, vitamins and cookery. She also found time to be a political speaker and television and radio personality.

She wrote her first book at the age of 21 and this was called *Jigsaw*. It became an immediate bestseller and sold 100,000 copies in hardback and was translated into 6 different languages. She wrote continuously throughout her life, writing bestsellers for an astonishing 76 years. Her books have always been immensely popular in the United States, where in 1976 her current books were at numbers 1 & 2 in the B. Dalton bestsellers list, a feat never achieved before or since by any author.

Barbara Cartland became a legend in her own lifetime and will be best remembered for her wonderful romantic novels, so loved by her millions of readers throughout the world.

Her books will always be treasured for their moral message, her pure and innocent heroines, her good looking and dashing heroes and above all her belief that the power of love is more important than anything else in everyone's life.

"I have always advised that you should never try too hard to find love or you will be disappointed. Love can come to you in a most unexpected way and at a most unlikely time. But do remember that out there somewhere is your great love and you will find each other."

Barbara Cartland

CHAPTER ONE
1866

As the train neared London, Lady Eleta Renton felt herself becoming more and more apprehensive.

She had never got on with her stepfather.

Therefore he would be extremely annoyed that she had been so long returning to England after leaving school.

She was already twenty and should have left when she was eighteen.

Eleta had, however, enormously enjoyed living in France and meeting so many girls from different countries.

She had stayed with a great number of her schoolfriends at their homes and, as she was so popular, they had hated her to leave them.

Her mother had died when she was seventeen and this was her third year as a pupil at the Convent of St. Mary Magdalene, which was just outside Paris.

It was in fact the most fashionable and certainly the most distinguished Finishing School in Europe and girls from fifteen onwards were taught by the nuns and every top professor in France.

It was very expensive, but even so many aristocrats in Europe felt their daughters should finish their education there and it would give them something special they could not obtain at any other school.

Eleta loved every single moment of her time at the Convent, especially learning foreign languages from other pupils.

She forced herself to talk in their language when she was alone with them and she soon became so fluent that she invariably won the Prize of the Year.

When her mother died, she happened to be staying in Africa with some French friends and it was impossible for her to return home in time for the funeral.

The Countess of Stanrenton had never been very strong after her daughter was born and spent a great deal of time with her doctors and it was not surprising to anyone when she died peacefully in her sleep.

When Eleta received the news from her stepfather, she was broken-hearted.

She adored her mother and could not bear to think that she had not been with her for the last days of her life.

There was, however, really no point in her hurrying back to England.

She had therefore sent a letter to her stepfather telling him that she was in Africa and that she would have another term at the Convent before coming home.

Actually it was over a year before she returned and, when she did, she found him even less attractive than he had been when her mother was alive.

So she had gone back to the Convent again and had stayed there enjoying every minute of it until now.

She would not have left even now if the Mother Superior had not said that she should go.

"You are now twenty, my dear," she said, "and the oldest girl here. I am sorry, but you really must leave us because there is nothing more we can teach you."

"Oh, don't say that, Reverend Mother," Eleta cried. "I feel I learn more and more every day I am here and I am very happy."

The Mother Superior knew the background only too well and why Eleta did not wish to return to her stepfather.

"I know and we would love to keep you. But we cannot break the rules of the Convent just for one girl."

"So I have to go back," Eleta replied in a low voice.

"You will find that you will soon enjoy yourself with your friends. Among the *debutantes* I am afraid you will find yourself really rather old and they will think you are 'not one of them,' so to speak."

Eleta had laughed.

The Mother Superior had said it in French using a slang expression.

"I will pray for you," the Mother Superior promised quietly, "and I know things will seem much better when you are at home than they do from here."

Eleta thought that she was being optimistic and it was most unlikely, but she had no choice except to leave at the end of the term.

It was now May and the sun was shining and she tried to think of how beautiful it would be at her father's house in Northamptonshire.

She realised, however, that she had to go to London first – to the house where her mother had died which was in Berkeley Square.

It was agony for her to think that her Mama would not be waiting for her as she always had been in the lovely drawing room filled with spring flowers.

The Countess would be sitting on the sofa with her feet up as her doctors had advised her to do and she would then hold out her arms as Eleta entered the room.

But now there would only be her stepfather.

She was quite certain that he would look at her in a way that she always disliked. It made her feel as if he was summing her up and not being pleased with the final sum.

The Earl of Stanrenton, Eleta's father, had died in a most unfortunate accident when he was out riding and his wife was broken-hearted and so was his daughter.

Eleta had adored and idolised her dear Papa, as she called him. Although he deeply regretted not having a son, he had been extremely fond of his pretty daughter.

It was two years later that the Countess had married again, simply because she was so lonely and depressed and also because Mr. Cyril Warner was very persuasive.

He was not an aristocrat as the Earl had been, but he had been well educated and had made a large fortune for himself building ships.

He was, however, as Eleta had discovered almost immediately, a tremendous snob.

He had not merely fallen in love with the widowed Countess, he had also thought being married to her was a huge step up on the social ladder for himself.

Eleta found during the holidays that her stepfather took endless pains to invite to the house anyone who had a title.

Eleta knew, although he had never said so, that he was deeply upset at not being able to have a child by his wife because she was not strong enough.

Therefore he had to be content with a stepdaughter.

But he was well aware that Eleta had resented him from the very moment he had married her mother.

It was not a happy situation and so Eleta spent a great deal of her holidays with her friends.

Only when her mother died quite suddenly did she bitterly regret that she had not been at home all the time.

She should have disregarded the fact that she was uncomfortable with her stepfather and resentful of him.

Now she thought despairingly, as her Mama was not there, she would have to see a great deal more of her stepfather than she had in the past.

She had already notified some of her friends that she was returning home and she was certain they would welcome her with open arms.

At the same time the house in Berkeley Square and Renton Park in the country would be incredibly dull and uncomfortable if she had to spend any time alone with her stepfather.

'If only Mama was here,' she thought, 'everything would be different.'

The mere thought of her Mama brought tears to her eyes and she had loved talking to her and being with her.

The Countess had been a most intelligent woman, despite having been brought up by Governesses and it was her idea that Eleta should have a better education than hers.

"I have had to teach myself," she admitted. "Your father was a great reader and an ardent traveller, so I learnt much from him. I must not now deprive you."

"I don't want to leave you," Eleta had said when she was told that she was to go to France.

"I will miss you, my darling," her mother replied, "more than I can say. But I know I am doing the right thing. You have the same intelligent brain as your father had, so you will learn from the Convent more than any Governess could possibly teach you."

So Eleta had gone to France unwillingly and had stayed longer than anyone expected, as she found that she was so happy there.

It was really fascinating not only to learn from the teachers at the Convent, but from all the girls themselves, especially those from distant countries.

Now, she thought, she had already seen a great deal of the world, but there was much more to see and she only hoped and prayed she would be able to go on travelling.

She was, however, anxious that her stepfather was already planning a social life for her and she knew in her heart of hearts that she would find it boring.

There would be endless balls every night to which inevitably she would be invited purely because she was her mother's and father's daughter.

And she was sure that her stepfather would insist on escorting her and that was because he would then meet the aristocrats whose daughters were the Season's *debutantes*.

'I am too old for *debutante* dances,' Eleta mused.

At the same time she knew that because there were always older people invited, she would not be particularly conspicuous.

In France it had not mattered if a girl was young or older. No one noticed if she was over or under eighteen if she could join in the conversation, if she could make men laugh and if she was beautiful.

Eleta had received a great many compliments from the French, but she thought on the whole that Englishmen were far more attractive.

She remembered listening to her father talking to her mother and it was not what he said but the note in his voice that revealed so clearly now much he loved her.

'What my Papa said were real compliments,' Eleta thought, 'but to the French they are just a normal part of conversation and mean very little.'

The train was now approaching London and once again she began to think of her stepfather waiting for her and of her Mama's empty bedroom.

'How could Mama have died and left me just when I wanted her so desperately?' Eleta reflected, as the train came steaming into the terminus.

Then she told herself that she must be nice to her stepfather because her mother had been fond of him. He had had made her happier than if she had remained alone.

When she looked out of the window, Eleta was glad to see it was not her stepfather who was waiting for her, but the secretary.

Mr. Melroy had looked after the accounts of the houses in London and in the country for her father.

When the train door opened and Eleta stepped out, she held out her hand to him.

"It's lovely to see you, Mr. Melroy," she said, "and very kind of you to come and meet me."

"I have been looking forward to your return, Lady Eleta," Mr. Melroy replied. "The house has seemed very dull without you and there is a warm welcome waiting for you from all the staff."

Eleta noticed that he did not include her stepfather.

She rode back in the carriage drawn by two well-trained horses, which had been her mother's favourites.

The coachman and the footman on the box were wearing the Stanrenton livery and it always proclaimed to Eleta all too firmly that her stepfather had no family livery.

'I must try to be nice to him for Mama's sake,' she told herself. 'Now she is not here, I only hope I don't have to be alone very often with Step-papa.'

The carriage drew up outside the house in Berkeley Square, which had belonged to her father's family for two generations and it was very comfortable and attractive.

As the carriage came to a standstill, two footmen wearing her father's livery laid the red carpet down on the pavement.

Because it was all so like home, Eleta jumped out and said, "hello, how are you?" to Harry.

"It's nice to 'ave you back, my Lady," Harry said.

Eleta walked into the hall and the butler, who had seemed old even when she was a baby, was waiting for her.

"Welcome, my Lady," he intoned. "It's been a long time and we've missed you."

"I have missed you too, Buxton," Eleta answered.

It was with difficulty she prevented herself from asking as she had asked so often before, 'where is Mama?'

As she hesitated, Buxton added,

"Mr. Warner's in the study, my Lady."

For a moment Eleta did not move.

Then she knew it would be rude if she went upstairs without at least telling her stepfather that she was back, so she walked towards the study.

The old butler quickly went ahead of her, opened the door and announced,

"Lady Eleta, sir."

Cyril Warner was seated at the writing table that had once been her father's.

It was a beautiful example of the Regency style and despite herself, because her Papa had always sat at it, Eleta resented seeing Cyril Warner in his place.

He rose slowly to his feet and held out his hand.

"So you are back at last," he began. "The ship must have been late."

"I thought we made up for it on the train," Eleta replied. "But the Channel was rougher than it usually is."

"Which it should not be at this time of the year," her Stepfather responded severely.

Buxton had stayed in the room.

"Will your Ladyship have tea in here," he asked, "or in the drawing room?"

Eleta looked at her stepfather and, before she could answer, he said,

"In here, Buxton. I wish to talk to her Ladyship and we must not be interrupted."

"Very good, sir."

He left the room and Cyril Warner moved to stand in front of the mantelpiece.

"It's a long time since you were at home," he said.

It was not just his words, but the way he said them which told Eleta that it was a rebuke.

"I am sorry, Step-papa, but as it so happens I was staying with friends in Greece and then with other friends in Cairo. Both visits were most enjoyable and instructive."

"I cannot think that they taught you anything you could not have learnt here in England," Cyril Warner said somewhat aggressively.

Eleta thought it was a mistake to argue.

He had always been against her being educated in France and he had at one time suggested that she came home and was taught by a Governess.

Her Mama, however, had resisted, knowing that she would learn more at the Convent than any Governess could teach her and so she had remained happily in France.

"Now I am here," Eleta said quickly, "I am very anxious to hear how things are in the country. Have you any new horses and are the flowers in the garden as lovely as I remember them?"

"The answer to your first question is 'no' and to your second, 'yes'," Cyril Warner answered abruptly.

Eleta was just about to protest that the horses when she last rode them were growing old when she remembered that he was not a good rider and did not particularly enjoy being on horseback.

So she changed the subject,

"I hope the old staff are still there and there are not too many newcomers."

"I have reduced the staff because I seldom go to the country," he replied. "I am in fact extremely busy. Busier than I have ever been before in London."

"How interesting," she managed to say. "Is it some new sort of ship you are building?"

She had just finished speaking as the door opened and Buxton came in with two footmen carrying the tea.

On a tray carried by the second footman there were large and small cakes that had been her favourites ever since she was a child.

One look at them told her that Mrs. Buxton was still in the kitchen and, as she walked over to the sofa to sit down in front of the tea tray, she said,

"Please tell Mrs. Buxton I am so glad that she has not forgotten me and I have been looking forward to her gingerbread ever since I left Calais."

"And the Missus has been working hard on all your Ladyship's best favourites and getting them ready since breakfast time this morning," Buxton replied.

"Do tell her I will come and see her when I have finished eating much more than I ought to," Eleta smiled.

"Now you enjoy yourself and don't worry about your weight," Buxton answered. "It's happy we all are to see your Ladyship back with us."

He left the room without waiting for Eleta's reply and she glanced at her stepfather to see him frowning.

'After all,' she reflected, 'it is my house and my home and everything in it was chosen by Mama or came from my father's family.'

Then she knew she was thinking of her stepfather once again as an intruder and she should not do it.

With an effort she asked,

"Do you like your tea, Step-papa, with or without milk or cream?"

"I want neither," Cyril Warner replied. "I just want to talk to you, Eleta."

He pulled up a chair and sat down on it facing her.

She had the sudden feeling that what he was going to say was something frightening, but she could not think what it could be.

She drew in her breath and felt an uncomfortable apprehension that she could not express in words.

She poured out her own cup of tea and then reached out to help herself from the nearest plate.

As she did so, she was aware that her stepfather was watching her and once again she had the feeling that there was something in his eyes or perhaps his silence that was almost sinister.

"What is it, Step-papa?" she asked him. "What has happened?"

"Nothing has happened, so far," he replied. "But it is something that I hope will happen quite soon."

"What is that?" Eleta enquired apprehensively.

She was thinking as she spoke that Mrs. Buxton's cooking had lost nothing with the passing of the years. In fact there were some new cakes on the table that she had not seen before but which she was anxious to sample.

"Now listen to me," her stepfather began.

"I am listening," Eleta replied. "At the same time it's so wonderful to be here and to have the same things to eat that I loved when I was a child and the same servants running the house as they have always done."

"I am glad you appreciate it," Cyril Warner said in a terse voice.

"I suppose we are all the same," Eleta sighed. "We enjoy ourselves when we are away, but it is wonderful to come home."

She was aware that Cyril Warner stiffened and then she asked,

"What is it? What are you trying to tell me?"

"I told you that I wanted to talk to you, Eleta. I therefore want your full attention."

"Of course that is what you will have. Equally you must not mind me enjoying my tea. Mrs. Buxton will be so upset if the plates go back untouched."

"I am not concerned with Mrs. Buxton's feelings one way or the other," he snapped. "And what I have to say concerns your future and that is much more important."

He spoke sharply and Eleta stared at him.

"Concerns my future," she repeated slowly. "What do you mean by that?"

"I mean that I have arranged your marriage and I am sure it will give you the same pleasure as it gives me."

"*My marriage*!" Eleta exclaimed. "What do you mean? How can you arrange my marriage?"

"Much more easily than I thought it would be," her Stepfather answered. "Unless living in France has made you less intelligent than I believe you to be, you will be delighted at what I have to tell you."

With a huge effort Eleta made herself ask slowly and in what she hoped was an ordinary voice,

"What have you arranged?"

Cyril Warner sat back in his chair.

"I have arranged that you will marry, as soon as possible, the Duke of Hazelware."

Eleta stared at him.

"You have arranged my marriage?" she questioned. "How could you possibly do that? I have never met the Duke of Hazelware. In fact I don't think that he was a friend of either my mother or my father."

"But he is a friend of mine and a most important one. He is in fact exactly the man I want as the Chairman of my new Company which he has promised to be. He will also benefit by having you as his wife. So that there is no reason for you to feel that he is condescending to you."

"I cannot imagine that what you are saying is true," Eleta cried. "Why should I marry the Duke of Hazelware whom I have never met? And it is not my concern whether he is Chairman of your Company or not."

Cyril Warner laughed and it was not a particularly pleasant sound.

"If you will allow me to explain the circumstances through which I obtained such a consequential husband for you," he said, "you will understand that it is a question of our both giving and receiving."

"What do you mean by that?" Eleta demanded.

"Well, I want an influential figure like the Duke as Chairman of my Company and he is anxious not only to have an heir, which he does not have at the moment, but also to be able to afford one."

Eleta stared at him.

"Are you then saying that the Duke is marrying me because I have my father's money, which I am well aware is very considerable?"

"That is the first intelligent remark you have made since you came home. As I have said, it's a question of give and take. While I want the Duke for my Company, he will benefit from the fact that you are a very lucky young woman in the matter of money."

"As you are referring to the money that belonged to my father and of course to my mother," Eleta said. "I have every intention of spending it, as they would want me to do on supporting those charities my mother was particularly interested in and in keeping up the estate which my father gave not only his money to but his love and attention."

"You are quite right and, with regard to the estate, the Duke will of course share it with you and will, I am sure, thanks to his vast experience, have many new ideas."

Eleta was silent for a moment and then she said,

"How old is this Duke?"

She knew as she spoke that it was a question he did not wish to answer and he looked uncomfortable, as Eleta continued,

"If you don't tell me the truth, I can easily look him up in *Debrett's Peerage* – there is one in the library."

"He is not a young man, of course he is not," her stepfather replied. "But he is, I am sure, very young in his outlook. Therefore you will benefit by his experience of life which you have not yet had."

"You have not answered my question," Eleta said quietly. "How old is the Duke we are talking about?"

Reluctantly and almost as if she had bullied it out of him, he replied after a long pause,

"Well, I think perhaps he is a little over fifty."

Eleta laughed.

"Do you really think that I would want to marry a man who is old enough to be my grandfather? The answer is quite simply '*no*'."

Cyril Warner sat back in his chair.

"Are you really so stupid, Eleta, as to think that is your final word?"

"Of course it's my final word. Have him on your Board, which I am sure is a very wise move, but I have no intention of marrying an old man and certainly not one who is marrying me for my money!"

There was silence for a moment and then he said,

"You have forgotten one thing."

"What can that be?" Eleta asked suspiciously

"That I am your Guardian by Law," her stepfather replied, "and you have to obey me until you are twenty-one. That, as I ascertained this morning, does not happen for nine months and by then you will be on my instructions married to the Duke of Hazelware."

Eleta stared at him.

"Do you really intend to force me up the aisle with someone I have no wish to marry, an old man who is marrying me for what I possess and not for myself?"

"All young women want a title," he replied.

"I already have a title and I have no wish to be a Duchess."

"Unfortunately or maybe fortunately," he answered, "the Duke is extremely necessary to me and I therefore can think of no other way to attract him than to offer him your hand in marriage."

"I think you must be mad if you believe I will agree to anything so ridiculous," Eleta stormed. "If my mother was alive, she would most certainly not allow you to even suggest anything quite so unpleasant to me."

"But, Eleta, your mother is not alive and I want to make it completely clear to you that I have gone into this very carefully. There is nothing you can do but obey me until you are twenty-one."

"I will not – " Eleta began, but he interrupted,

"It is then you will have complete control over your fortune and yourself. But until then you have to obey your Guardian by Law and I, at present, hold that position."

He spoke as if he was addressing a crowd of stupid and uneducated people and there was an expression in his eyes and in the tone of his voice that told Eleta all too clearly that he meant to have his own way.

She realised, because she was extremely intelligent, that she was at the moment at a complete disadvantage.

If she defied the law, she would have no support and would finally have to agree to his outrageous idea.

She wanted to scream and she wanted to hit him.

She wanted to fight for her freedom.

But she knew that she was powerless to do so.

She therefore slowly and deliberately cut herself a piece of cake and put it on her plate before she said,

"I must say, Step-papa, that this is a great shock to me as soon as I have arrived home. Perhaps we should go into more detail and you could explain to me more fully why the Duke has come into our lives or rather into my life without my having met him."

"But of course you will meet him," Cyril Warner replied, "but he is in the Midlands at the moment where he has a dilapidated castle which is urgently in need of repair, but he should be back tomorrow or the day after."

"You think that he will then make me a proposal of marriage?" Eleta managed to say.

"He has already told me that he is delighted at the idea of marrying someone young, beautiful and of course with a large fortune"

He paused, but as Eleta did not speak he continued,

"He was married at one time, but his wife died without giving him any children and he has not been able to afford to be in London often lately."

He gave a snide laugh before he added,

"He has managed, I think with some difficulty, to remain a bachelor."

"I suppose you want him on some new project?"

"I want him badly," her stepfather answered. "Not that he knows anything about ships or the material which goes into them, but his name will mean a great deal to me and to those who work with me."

Cyril Warner's voice rose sharply as he added,

"As you must know, all Dukes are deeply respected in this country and abroad, especially in America."

There was a note in his voice that told Eleta far better than words that America was where the Duke would shine. If he was to represent her stepfather's products, they would automatically be of great interest to the Americans.

There was silence for a moment, then Eleta said,

"And the Duke can do this without involving me."

"Sadly the truth is that His Grace is exceedingly hard-up. I have not yet visited his ancestral home, which is in Nottinghamshire, but I am told it is in urgent need of repair which he cannot afford."

He seemed to Eleta to glare at her as he went on,

"The cost of restoring it to what it was a hundred years ago will mean little to you, but it should be a great satisfaction when you become the reigning Duchess with an estate which is as perfect as your father made his estate in Northamptonshire."

"Which is mine," Eleta asserted. "What will happen to it if I am busy, as you suggest, in Nottinghamshire?"

"I am sure with all the education you have had," her Stepfather replied sarcastically, "two estates will not be too much for you and you should be able to manage them as competently as your mother managed this house."

"I think perhaps, Step-papa, that you are being very optimistic, but naturally I would like to see His Grace's house before I commit myself one way or another."

"You would be wasting your time – "

He was almost shouting the words at her and he continued,

"You will marry the Duke as soon as it is possible to arrange the marriage. Because we will need to make everyone aware of such a splendid occasion, it must take place immediately. At the beginning of next month would be best, just before the Royal Ascot races."

"I see you have arranged everything," Eleta said. "But you must understand my feelings."

She was about to say much more, but her stepfather broke in, almost snarling the words,

"You have to marry the Duke and I cannot wait for you to have airs and graces about it. You will marry him when I can arrange a date with him as soon as he arrives here. All you have to do is to spend a considerable amount of money on a wedding gown, which must be outstanding, and of course we can invite at least five hundred people if we use the garden in the centre of the Square."

From the way he spoke, Eleta was aware that he had planned every move and there would be little point in her arguing.

She therefore rose from the tea table and stipulated,

"As I have been travelling since early this morning, you will understand that I must now go upstairs and rest."

"I have a great many more things to say to you," he replied. "You must therefore make an effort to come down to dinner. I have your mother's list of friends who must all be invited and you must have made many friends at your school and they too should receive an invitation."

"Yes, Step-papa, I understand, but I really am very tired and you must forgive me if I go now and lie down."

She walked across the room as she was speaking, but he made no effort to rise or to open the door for her.

He merely watched her with what she thought were suspicious eyes as she walked out of the room.

She deliberately closed the door quite quietly and then she forced herself to walk to the hall and up the stairs.

There were two footmen on duty there and, as she had not seen them before, she greeted them and they said that they were glad to see her back.

As she reached her room, she found the old lady's maid, who had looked after her mother, waiting for her.

Because it was a familiar voice and brought back memories of her childhood, Eleta kissed her warmly.

"If there is anyone I was hoping to see here when I returned home, it is you, Betty."

"I was hopin' you'd not forget me, my Lady."

Betty was now in late middle-age and her hair was going grey, but, when she smiled, Eleta thought it was the same smile she remembered Betty giving her in the cradle.

"Oh, Betty, I am thankful you are here," Eleta said. "I suppose you have some idea of what my stepfather has been saying to me."

"We all knows he's determined that you'll marry the Duke," Betty replied.

"How could he think I would do such a thing?"

"I was wonderin' that meself, my Lady, but you knows what the Master be like. He never ever listens to anythin' he don't want to hear."

"I know that," Eleta said, "which is why I stopped arguing with him, but you can be sure that I will not marry the Duke and no law will force me."

She spoke with a violence that had not been in her voice when she was downstairs.

Betty looked at her, then hurried across the room to make quite certain that the door was shut before saying,

"I knew you'd feel like this, my Lady, but what can you do?"

"What I have every intention of doing," Eleta said slowly, "is to run away!"

CHAPTER TWO

Betty stared at her.

"Run away?" she repeated.

"Yes. How can I do – anything else? You know as well as I do, I cannot marry a man I have never seen – who is old and is marrying me – only because I am rich."

The words seemed to tumble from her lips.

"Now don't you upset yourself, my Lady. I know it's terrible, but you've got to think it out."

"I've thought it out already. I intend to run away as quickly as I can and will never, never come back here until Step-papa is thinking very differently."

Betty put her hand up to her face.

"You can't do it, my Lady, you're too pretty and far too young to be alone anywhere."

Eleta was still for a moment. She knew that Betty was right and it would be very difficult for her to go to any of her friends. If she did so, she was certain her stepfather would find her and drag her away.

There was silence as both of them were thinking and then finally Eleta exclaimed,

"There must be something I can do, somewhere I can go."

"If I'd a home," Betty said, "it'd be there for you as long as you'd want it."

Eleta smiled at her.

"I know that, dearest Betty, and I would trust you, while I wouldn't trust anyone else not to tell Step-papa where I was, however much he offered you."

She spoke bitterly, thinking that money was all that mattered and so the Duke would marry her without even seeing her, simply because she was rich.

Because she felt she could not sit still, she stood up and walked to the window.

"What can I do? What on earth can I do?" she asked desperately.

There was only silence from Betty and then after a moment Eleta suggested,

"I wonder, I just wonder, if I found a job as a Governess, whether that would prove a hiding-place? I am sure it is something Step-papa would not expect me to do."

"I'm afraid, my Lady, that no one'd take such a young Governess or such a pretty one. You'll remember what your Governesses looked like when they was here."

Eleta recalled that they had been middle-aged and dull. They had taught her very little, which was why her mother had insisted she went to the Convent School.

"You are quite right, Betty, I don't look like them and I don't want to!"

"Of course not, but then you might find somethin' if you went to the Agency."

Eleta started.

"I did not think of that. They might have all sorts of unusual jobs. After all I speak a good few languages."

"It's just an idea, because you're too young and too pretty and too much a Lady to find work easily."

"It seems unfair, but, if I had a face like the back of a cab, there would doubtless be a dozen jobs for me to do!"

"But the Almighty's made you as pretty as your mother and you should thank Him on your knees for that."

"I am more than prepared to thank Him, but it's obviously a handicap where a job is concerned."

"I'm sure we can think of somethin'," Betty went on. "I'd be so much happier if you was in a decent house and sleepin' in a comfortable bed than if you was hidin' yourself in lodgings or somewhere like that."

Eleta knew what she meant and she was intelligent enough to realise that she could easily be the prey of any man who fancied her.

She recognised that if she was alone she would be frightened and, if she did find a job working in a school or even a shop, she would still have to accommodate herself at night and that was where the danger would be.

"Should we go to the Agency, Betty, and find out what is available? I suppose there is one round here."

"Of course there's one, my Lady. It's where your Mama always went if she wanted a housemaid or someone extra to work in the kitchen."

"Then come with me, Betty, and we'll go there and see what happens."

"We'll have to walk," Betty replied.

"Of course!" Eleta agreed, not having thought of it herself. "I think too we had better wait until Step-papa has gone out. He is certain to go back to his office and then I will not have him pouncing on me again."

She spoke bitterly and Betty put out her hand and laid it on Eleta's shoulder.

"Now don't you go talkin' like that. We'll find a way out of this mess, but I can't have you speakin' as your mother never did and I know it'd hurt her."

Eleta smiled.

"You are quite right, Betty. This is a very difficult situation, but somehow I will find a way out of it. I will try not to be bitter, which would have upset Mama."

"That's right. Now wait here while I pop out to see what's happenin'. And you'd best change into somethin' plain and serviceable if you're really goin' to the Agency."

"You are quite right. I had not thought of that."

Betty left and Eleta went to her wardrobe.

She took out a plain coat and skirt she had worn at school and put it on, together with a pair of flat shoes.

Then she hesitated.

Most of her hats were elaborately ornate with many flowers and ribbons and they would look very out of place.

Then she remembered that when she was riding she often wore a plain felt hat with a brim. It was especially useful when the sun was hot and it shaded her eyes.

It took her some moments to find it.

Her clothes from Paris had not all been unpacked and finally she discovered it folded flat at the bottom of one of her hat-boxes.

She put it on her head after pulling back her curly fair hair and pinning it tidily in place and, when she looked in the mirror, she laughed.

She certainly did not look like herself, but at the same time it was no use pretending that she did not still look very attractive and very young.

Betty came back after quite a time.

"The Master's just left," she said, "and I heard him givin' a message to Mr. Buxton that he wanted to see you when he returns."

"At any rate he has gone for the moment," Eleta said, "so we can leave as soon as you are ready."

Betty looked at her quizzically

"If you asks me, they'll think it strange downstairs if you appear in that get-up."

"But what can I do, Betty, unless I jump out of the window?"

"Then we'll go out the back way, my Lady. When they've finished in the kitchen, Mrs. Buxton lies down and those who help her goes shoppin'."

Eleta spread out her hands.

"I will leave it to you, Betty, to get me out of this house without anyone being suspicious of my appearance. The last thing I want when I do disappear is for them to tell Step-papa that I did not look like myself."

"I'll get my bonnet," Betty said. "I won't be long."

She hurried away and Eleta went along the corridor to her mother's bedroom.

It was just as she had left it. Only the flowers were missing, which had always scented the room and made it look even lovelier than it already was.

As soon as Eleta walked through the door, she was aware of the fragrant smell of violets. It was the scent her mother always used and had been her father's favourite.

When Eleta shut her eyes, she could almost believe that her Mama was either lying in the bed or sitting on the sofa by the windows.

'Help me, Mama, do help me,' she begged silently. 'You know I cannot marry this horrible man whom Step-papa has found for me. So help me! Help me disappear until he gives up this awful idea.'

She felt her whole being reach out to her Mama.

Then somehow she felt her mother answering her and telling her not to worry. And she could almost see her smiling at her as she had always done and Eleta knew that whatever else might happen to her, her mother was there thinking of her and loving her.

Almost as if she was being directed by her Mama, Eleta was suddenly aware that if she went to an Agency she would need references.

She sat down at the beautiful French secretaire in the corner of the room and opened the drawers.

There was the writing paper her mother had always used with the Family Crest die-stamped on it.

Eleta thought for a moment that she could not use it and then she asked herself why not?

She would have to apply under an assumed name and there was no reason why her mother could not have employed her in the past.

She therefore wrote quickly,

"The Countess of Stanrenton is very pleased to recommend as a Governess – "

Eleta hesitated and then continued,

"Miss *Ellen Lawson, who I have employed for the past three years and has proved most satisfactory.*

She is very intelligent, speaks several languages and has carried out her work in a conscientious manner.

In fact the Countess cannot speak too highly of Miss Lawson and is prepared to give her a reference at any time she needs one."

Eleta read what she had written and she thought it was just the sort of thing her mother would have said in giving a reference to anyone she was fond of.

That, she thought, was one reference at any rate.

She looked in the drawer, as she wanted to see if there was by chance a piece of writing paper with another address on it.

Then she noticed stacked tidily in a corner some writing paper from a hotel, one her parents had stayed in when they thought the sea air would do them good.

She tried to make her handwriting look different and wrote a glowing reference from a lady she invented who was currently staying in the hotel.

She said that she had employed Miss Lawson only temporarily while she was in England and had found her excellent. Her French was Parisian and as good as she would expect to find in any French girl of the same age.

She signed the letter with a French name and on the top of it she made the writer a Comtesse.

As Eleta folded up the two letters, she thanked her Mama silently for helping her. She was almost sure that she was smiling and telling her not to be worried.

She went back to her bedroom expecting to find Betty there, but she did not arrive for another ten minutes.

Then she came bursting into the room dressed in the black bonnet and black cape she always went out in.

"Come along then, my Lady," she said, "the coast's clear, Mrs. Buxton's gone to rest and the kitchen's empty."

"I was afraid you had forgotten about me," Eleta said jokingly.

"You know I'd never forget you," Betty answered. "You mean more to me than if you were my own child and I'd help you if I could even with my dying breath."

"I know you would, Betty," Eleta said and, bending forward, kissed her cheek. "Now come along, we have to think of this as a new adventure and I must not make any mistakes or I will find myself back here and married before I can say 'Jack Robinson'."

"God forbid that should happen!" Betty exclaimed.

They went down by the staircase which led to the back of the premises and out through the basement door from which there were steps into Berkeley Square.

Then they hurried out and into Davis Street, just in case a footman was looking out from the front door.

They did not speak until they were out of sight of the house and then Betty drew a deep breath.

"I don't think anyone noticed us," she sighed.

"I am sure that they didn't and thank you, Betty, for being clever enough to remember that is the best way to leave the house when one does not wish to be seen."

"I hadn't thought of it before and that's the truth!"

"Now where is this Agency you have been talking about?" Eleta asked.

"It's not far, my Lady, it's just at the back of these shops and convenient for them as wants staff locally."

They walked on in silence until they came to what looked like an ordinary house, but the front door was open revealing a narrow staircase.

"It's on the first floor," Betty said unnecessarily, "and I'll be waiting for you here."

"You are not coming with me?" Eleta asked.

Betty shook her head.

"They knows me because I've been here once or twice for your mother when she wanted a kitchenmaid. Mrs. Hill, that be her name, might recognise me and that'd be unhelpful."

Eleta knew this was common sense, so she said,

"Don't go far away, Betty."

"I'll wait at the end of the street. There's no hurry and be careful where you promises to go."

Eleta smiled at her.

"I'll be careful, I promise, Betty. Now pray hard that I will find a place I can hide from Step-papa."

"I'll be prayin'," Betty assured her.

Then, as if worried she might be seen, she walked off leaving Eleta alone outside the open door,

She walked up the narrow stairs.

At the top the door was open and she saw inside what looked like servants sitting on chairs against the wall.

There were three young girls she thought must be housemaids or perhaps kitchenmaids. And several young men she was certain were looking for jobs with horses.

As they stared at her, she saw at the far end of the room that there was a high desk and seated at it was an elderly woman with grey hair and wearing glasses.

On the desk there was a large book and in front of her was a woman who was obviously asking for a job.

As she stood wondering if she should sit down, the woman turned away and started to walk towards the door.

Obviously she was now leaving and Eleta decided to speak to Mrs. Hill before anyone else did, so, walking slowly as if in no hurry, she approached the desk.

Mrs. Hill was making a note in the book and so did not look up until Eleta reached her and then she asked in a somewhat affected voice,

"Who are you?"

"My name is Ellen Lawson and – I am hoping, Mrs. Hill, that you could – find me a place as a Governess."

"As a Governess!" Mrs. Hill exclaimed. "You look too young to be teaching children and that's a fact."

"I am older than I look," Eleta answered. "And I do speak a number of languages fluently including French, German, Spanish and Greek."

Mrs. Hill regarded at her as if she thought that she was joking and then she laughed.

"There are not many children in Mayfair who want to learn all that," she said.

"Perhaps I could be a secretary in an Embassy."

Eleta had only just thought of that idea and then she wondered why she had not done so before.

"Embassies usually take on people from their own countries," Mrs. Hill said, "and they seldom come asking me for staff."

There was a note in her voice that told Eleta it was a sore point, so she therefore persevered quietly,

"I would be very glad of a position. As I have said, preferably with children or as a secretary to anyone who has to deal with foreign countries."

"If you mean businessmen, you will find them hard task-masters and mean on the cash. In fact to be honest I don't encourage them to come here looking for staff."

Eleta was silent. She felt that Mrs. Hill was being hostile and she would then have to think of another way of escaping from her stepfather.

Then unexpectedly a woman she had not noticed put her head in sight. She obviously had been listening to the conversation and was working behind another desk.

"What about the Marquis?" she asked almost in a whisper.

"I had not thought of him," Mrs. Hill replied. "In fact I had forgotten he was back on our books again."

"For the umpteenth time," the other woman joked, "and you can be certain it'll not be the last!"

Eleta was listening intently and, as Mrs. Hill was hesitating, she said,

"I am very experienced and I should have given you these the moment I arrived."

She handed over the two references she had written herself and Mrs. Hill took them from her and read them.

Then she said,

"I do remember the Countess. It wasn't very often they changed their staff. A very kind Lady she was, which is more than I can say for some of them as live in Berkeley Square."

"I was very happy with her until she died."

"I can well believe that. You can take my word for it, it's the best that go first and we're left with the worst!"

Mrs. Hill read the second letter again.

"Why have you left this Lady?" she asked.

"She has gone back to France and since I have been in France for some years I want to be in England now."

"I can understand that," Mrs. Hill replied. "When it comes down to it, there's nowhere like home."

"That is why I am hoping you will be able to find me somewhere here," Eleta added.

Mrs. Hill's assistant piped up.

"It's no use, she will have to go to the Marquis and we can only hope she'll stay longer than the last two did."

"Who is this Marquis," Eleta asked, "and why does he change his staff so frequently?"

"You may have heard of him. He's the Marquis of Teringford and it's his child who gives us more trouble than anyone else."

"His child?" Eleta questioned.

"There's not one woman in a million who can stand her goings-on," the assistant said. "And they comes back here saying if they was paid all the money in China they wouldn't stay another day with her."

31

"Now don't put Miss Lawson off before she's even begun," Mrs. Hill came back sharply. "We've no one else to send, Gertie, so stop making it even more difficult."

As if rebuked, Gertie disappeared behind the desk.

"We've been looking after the Marquis's staff for some years," Mrs. Hill said. "There's nothing wrong with the Marquis, it's his daughter who's the trouble.

"Is she a child?" Eleta asked.

"She's a child all right, just nine years of age and, if you ask me, she's a real horror. At the same time she's the Marquis's daughter and we have to find her a Governess, although Heaven knows where we can find another one."

"I told you, if you remember," Eleta said quietly, "I want to be a Governess, but you said I was too young."

"Well, you certainly look too young to me," Mrs. Hill replied, as if to justify herself. "But the post's open at the moment if you would like to try your hand at it. I must be honest, seeing as you've got such good references."

"What is wrong?" Eleta enquired.

"You would think a child of nine would be easy to handle, but she's set herself against any form of learning and Governess after Governess has failed to make her even learn the alphabet, let alone anything else."

Eleta could hardly believe that this was true.

"What is wrong with the child?"

"There's nothing wrong at all as far as her health's concerned. The Marquis is a charming man, but he can no more control his daughter than turn back the tide."

"It sounds very strange to me," Eleta said. "But I am prepared to try my hand at teaching the child and – who knows – I might succeed where the others have failed."

"I'll give you a medal for valour if you do," Mrs. Hill answered. "Isn't that true, Gertie?"

The assistant put her head round the desk again.

"I wouldn't bet on anyone succeeding where that child's concerned, but let Miss Lawson have a go. There's no one else on our books at present as you well know."

Mrs. Hill hesitated for a moment.

"Well, you'll be doing us a big favour as well as yourself. If you succeed, all I can say is that I'll bless you from the top of your head to the soles of your feet!"

Eleta laughed.

"That does sound very encouraging and I can only promise that you I will do my best. But do tell me a little more about the Marquis and his daughter."

"He's a very nice gentleman and I'm sorrier for him than I am for anyone else. His wife died having this child and I've heard, although it may not be true, that he's sworn he'll never marry again.

"There's plenty ready to wear the Teringford jewels if only he'd ask them. It's a real shame that young man who's lost his wife should have a child like his."

"Where does he live?" Eleta asked, hoping it was not in London.

"He's got a house in Hertfordshire which I'm told is one of the finest and most impressive houses in England. He also has a big mansion in Park Lane and, when he gives parties, I read about them in *The Court Circular* and the smart people of London are his guests."

"So his daughter is in the country?" Eleta asked.

She wanted to make sure that she would not have to be in London, as Park Lane was too near to her own home.

"Yes, the child is in the country and you'd think she'd be happy there with her father's horses. It's only fair to tell you that we've sent no less than five Governesses

33

who've all come back and said they'd rather starve than put up with that child for another moment."

"Don't put her off having a try," Gertie cautioned.

"You are not putting me off," Eleta came in. "I am perfectly willing to have a go and I only hope for your sake as well as mine that I will be successful."

"It'll be a miracle if you are," Mrs. Hill said, "but don't say I haven't warned you."

"If I crawl back, you must not laugh at me!"

"I certainly won't do that. I'd give you a crown if I had one, but my grateful thanks will cost nothing. I only swear I'll find you another job if you give up on this one."

"Thank you very much," Eleta sighed, "and I am very very grateful."

"When can you go there?" Mrs. Hill asked her.

"What would suit me best is to leave late tonight. It may perhaps be rather inconvenient, but I am obliged, for reasons I don't wish to discuss, to leave the place where I am staying at the moment."

"That'll be difficult," Mrs. Hill said after thinking it over. "What you could do, if you could manage it, is to go early tomorrow morning. It'll give me a chance to inform his Lordship's secretary that he must provide you with a proper conveyance."

Eleta had not thought of this, but she could see it was sensible.

"Very well," she said, "I will be here at six o'clock tomorrow morning. And if I then have to wait for the conveyance, perhaps you would be kind enough to have someone let me in."

"It seems to me," Mrs. Hill remarked in a different tone of voice, "that you are escaping from somewhere."

"You are very clever," Eleta replied. "The people I am with now don't wish to lose me, but I have to leave them for a number of reasons. I therefore want to get away without a scene, either late tonight or very early tomorrow morning, whichever you think the most convenient."

"Well, I tell you what I'll do. Neither of us want to get up as early as six o'clock. So if I give you a spare key to the door, you can sit there until the carriage arrives."

"That is very kind," Eleta said. I promise not to be a nuisance and I will lock the door when I leave and push the key through the letterbox."

"That seems safe to me, but you haven't asked me yet, Miss Lawson, what wages you'll be wanting."

"No, I forgot about that," Eleta replied.

"You won't get far in life if you don't see that they pay you properly," Mrs. Hill said in a rebuking tone. "At the same time you've struck lucky where that's concerned as His Lordship's very generous. He realises, as we do, it's not an easy position and in my view it never will be."

"That's putting it mildly," Gertie added. "If you asks me, I'd want a thousand pounds a day for that child!"

"Now *you* are putting Miss Lawson off, Gertie."

Eleta laughed,

"Don't worry, she is not putting me off. I do rather like difficult problems and surely this is a most difficult one. So I will enjoy trying to do what other people have failed to accomplish."

"All I can say is you're different from most folk," Mrs. Hill replied somewhat tartly.

She handed Eleta a card with the name and address of where she had to go and then another card on which was written her monthly salary.

And that she was entitled to four weeks holiday during the year and one day off a week provided she could find someone in the household to look after Lady Priscilla.

That, she realised, was the Marquis of Teringford's daughter and the wages were much larger than anything her mother had ever paid her Governess.

She knew therefore that, if he was willing to pay so much, the Marquis must be desperate in trying to find a Governess.

She put the two cards into her handbag and said,

"Thank you very much for all your kindness and I promise I will do my best for your sake as well as my own in trying to stay where the others have all left."

She held out her hand and, as if it was somewhat unusual, Mrs. Hill seemed surprised as she took it.

"You will not forget to order the carriage and give me the key," she said.

"Of course not. Here it is and you won't forget to put it through the letterbox will you?"

"I will not forget," Eleta promised. "I hope that the carriage will not be late for me."

She knew as she spoke it was going to be difficult to get away, but it was a chance in a million.

Wherever her stepfather might look for her, she was certain it would not occur to him that she was a Governess.

Yet because he was so fond of titles he might, she suddenly thought, wonder if she had found a situation in any of their houses.

Just for a moment she was frightened and then she remembered that she had changed her name.

It was not likely that her stepfather would admit to the people he was impressed by that his stepdaughter had run away and was hiding from him.

'I am sure I am safe. I must be,' she told herself as she walked down the stairs.

She could see Betty not far away and ran towards her excitedly.

"I have won! I have won!" she cried. "I have been given a situation as a Governess and I can only pray, Betty, that I can keep it."

"You've got a situation!" Betty exclaimed.

"Let's sit down somewhere so that I can tell you all about it," she suggested.

"We'll go to the Park. No one'll listen to us there."

They walked quickly towards Hyde Park and found an empty seat under some trees.

"Now tell me exactly what's happened, my Lady. I promise you, I've been prayin' that you'd find somewhere decent to go."

"It sounds a most difficult place from what Mrs. Hill said," Eleta answered. "But I am engaged and they are picking me up very early tomorrow morning."

"Who are you going to?" Betty asked. "I hope it's somewhere respectable and you won't get into trouble."

"It's not likely except from my pupil. Apparently she is responsible for a number of Governesses leaving."

"Who is she and why should she do so?"

"She is the daughter of the Marquis of Teringford."

For a moment Betty just stared at her and then she said,

"Oh, not him! You can't go to him, my Lady, that be impossible!"

CHAPTER THREE

Eleta stared at Betty.

"What do you mean?" she asked her. "Why should I not go to the Marquis's house?"

Betty was silent and Eleta knew she was struggling to find the right words and then she began,

"I've heard a great deal about that Marquis because a friend of mine worked there at one time. She tells me about him, which I thinks you should hear."

"But of course I want to hear it. If I am to teach his daughter, the more I know about him the better. It's so like you, Betty, to know about a man I have never heard of."

"I'm real sure that your mother would have known about him and of course your father. But, as they didn't approve of him, he were not invited to Berkeley Square."

"They did not approve of him? But why?"

"Let's start at the beginning. My friend tells me he were only nineteen when he married. He fell in love with a very pretty girl and, as he were to become a Marquis, her family was delighted they should be married."

"Was she the same age as him?" Eleta asked.

"No, a bit younger, she was in fact only seventeen, getting on for eighteen, and all the newspapers, as you can imagine, made a good story of the bride and bridegroom being so young and aristocratic."

"So the bride also came from a good family?"

"Her father was an Earl and she therefore had a courtesy title," Betty replied, "as her bridegroom had."

"So they were married," Eleta said, feeling that the story was rather slow in coming out.

"They were then married and I hears they was very happy, but sadly the bride died having a baby."

"Yes, I was told that at Mrs. Hill's. It was dreadful. Was the Marquis broken-hearted?"

"I was told he was at first, but afterwards, perhaps because he wanted to forget, he began to enjoy himself."

"What do you mean by that, Betty?"

"Well, he pursued all the most beautiful women in London and the gossips talked about him day and night."

"But he did not get married again?"

"No, he be very careful not to do that. My friend said he were so unhappy when his wife died that he vowed never to marry or get involved with an unmarried woman."

Eleta stared at her.

"Are you saying, Betty, that the women he had 'affairs' with, if that's what you mean, were all married?"

"All of them and it gives him a very bad name. It were whispered that one husband threatened to challenge him to a duel, but, as it were forbidden by Her Majesty, they ended up by having a fist-fight that most unfairly, it's thought, the Marquis won."

Eleta then laughed as it sounded so funny and Betty continued,

"It's said in Mayfair among the grand hostesses that no one's safe when that Marquis is prowlin' about."

Eleta laughed again.

"I suppose it's what you might expect if he is as good-looking as you say he is and very rich too."

"I am sure of that at any rate," Betty said. "He has horses that win races and a big house in Hertfordshire."

"That is where I have to go tomorrow."

"Over my dead body! I'm not havin' you run after by someone who's whispered about by every respectable Lady in the country. You go straight back to Mrs. Hill and tell her to find somewhere else. You're far too pretty, my Lady, to be under the same roof as that man!"

Betty was speaking very seriously and Eleta knew that she was worried because she loved her.

She put out her hand and laid it over Betty's.

"Now listen to me, Betty. I love you for caring for me and being worried, as I know Mama would worry."

"Your dear mother wouldn't allow you to go to the home of a roué and a man who's talked about as much as that Marquis is and that's the truth."

"If Mama was here," Eleta replied, "she would not allow Step-papa to marry me to an old decrepit Duke who only wants me because I have money.

"But I have to escape and I have to do it quickly. You know how determined Step-papa is when he wants anything and I will find myself married before I know it."

Betty wanted to speak, but Eleta went on quickly,

"I love you for worrying about me, but you must realise, as you have said, that the Marquis is determined not to marry again."

"He's not likely to ask you anyway, my Lady, as you're only a Governess, to marry him," Betty conceded.

"I know that," Eleta replied, "but I am also aware from what you have said that he is so frightened of being married again that he never even looks at young girls, only married women, whom he cannot marry."

She thought that she had not put it very clearly, but Betty understood what she was saying and relaxed a little.

"That be true," she said. "But my friend says he's never taken any girl to his house in the country nor even to his house in London."

"That is just what I was saying, Betty."

"But you're so pretty like your mother, there must be dozens of other houses you can go to rather than his."

"There may be dozens of them, but the only one on Mrs. Hill's books was the Marquis's and they don't really expect me to stay there more than a few days."

"I've heard about that. The child's unmanageable and my friend says she's had more Governesses than any other child she'd ever heard of."

"Did she say what was wrong with her, Betty?"

"She didn't think there were anythin' wrong except that she be very naughty. Perhaps the first Governess she had upset her, but she just refuses to learn."

"Nothing?" Eleta asked.

"Nothin' at all. She screams and cries if they try to make her do her lessons and the last Governess my friend heard of says she's a child of Satan and un-teachable!"

Eleta laughed.

"She certainly sounds most unusual. So how old is the little monster?"

As she asked the question, she remembered Mrs. Hill saying that she was only nine years of age and before Betty could reply, she went on,

"It's just ridiculous to say that a child of nine is un-teachable and, if you ask me, the Governesses must have been very stupid women."

"Now you really don't want to put yourself in an unpleasant position to then get the sack," Betty suggested.

"From what I've heard, some of the Governesses walked out even before they'd met the Marquis."

"It all sounds absurd, like something in a book. If I only stay there two days, it will be a new experience and different from anything I have ever encountered before."

She was thinking of the Convent, where the girls automatically always obeyed the nuns and were in awe of the Mother Superior.

"How is it possible," she asked, "that one small child could defeat properly trained Governesses?"

"Whatever you may say or think," Betty persisted, "I'm not happy about your goin' there."

"I am not happy about going anywhere, but I have to hide from my stepfather and I cannot imagine it would enter his head that I should want to become a Governess or a servant of any sort."

"Perhaps he'll send for the Police when he finds you're not in the house," Betty murmured.

"I doubt it. The one thing he will not want is a scandal of any sort. It would certainly set Mayfair talking if they knew I had run away the day after I had returned from school."

"That's true," Betty agreed.

"Also, what could Step-papa say if people asked him why I had disappeared in such a strange manner?"

There was no answer to this and, after a moment's silence, Eleta said,

"No, what he will do perhaps is to engage a Private Detective to try to find me or just make enquiries himself amongst my friends. There's a list of them, as he knows, in Mama's address book. But even so he will have to be very careful or they will talk and wonder where I can be."

"I still don't like your goin' to that man, whatever you may say," Betty muttered.

"I know, Betty, but I have to get away at once and I cannot think of any better way of disappearing than going to a grand house in the country where Step-papa has never been invited."

Betty gave a deep sigh as she was, as Eleta knew, defeated. She was aware that whatever she might say Eleta would still do what she wanted to do.

"Now you have to be helpful and we both have to be very clever, Betty. I have to leave home early tomorrow morning and be waiting outside the Agency at six o'clock.

"What about your luggage, my Lady?"

"That is where you have to help me tonight."

"Tonight?" she questioned. "What do you mean?"

"I am going home to pack up everything I require and I want you to take it round to the Agency and put it on the stairs just inside the front door."

"That's clever of you, I grant you that."

"I thought you would, Betty, and of course I must take enough clothes with me to last me for perhaps a long time before Step-papa sees sense."

"And you expect me to tell you when he does."

"Of course. You know, dearest Betty, I will tell you exactly what I am doing and, if I do leave the Marquis's house, you will have to help me find another position."

"You know I'll do that, my Lady, but I don't like your goin' there in the first place."

"I have no alternative, so we just have to accept things as they are and not as we want them to be."

Eleta rose from the bench and proposed,

43

"Now we will go home and start packing, but be very careful what you say to me just in case any of the housemaids are listening.

"There is just one other thing I want you to do for me now, Betty. I want you to go to my bank in Dover Street. It will only take you a very short time to get there."

"I suppose you want me to draw out some money," Betty said, "and that's real sensible of you."

"It will be quite a large sum and you must explain, if they query it, that I am going on a long journey abroad and that is why I need so much."

"They'll not ask the Master before they give it to you?" Betty enquired.

"No, it's my own money in my own name, but I think it would be a mistake to go myself to the bank."

They were now walking back through Grosvenor Square and Eleta was thinking of what she must do.

'I must be practical about this,' she told herself. 'I must not do something stupid which might result in Step-papa finding me.'

At the house Eleta went up to her room, found her chequebook and wrote a cheque for five hundred pounds.

Then she put it in an envelope and gave it to Betty.

"If I need more money," she said, "I will have my chequebook with me. But to make sure that the bank does not know where it has come from, I will send the cheque to you to cash it for me."

"I think this should last you for some time," Betty commented. "It's a lot of money and don't you waste it or get it stolen."

"I promise to do neither, Betty. As you know I've always tried to keep my promise."

"That be true enough, but you're going to live a very different life from the one you've lived before."

"I know that, which is why, Betty dear, I need your help. It's a great comfort to me to know that whatever occurs you are here and will let me know what happens."

"I'll do that," Betty promised. "But I wish you was goin' to any other house rather than that man's."

"Now you are making it sound even more exciting than it already is!"

"You must promise me one thing," Betty said. "If he makes advances to you, you then come straight home. You'll be better off with the Duke, old though he may be, than with that Marquis."

"I have my doubts about that for the simple reason that the Duke is offering marriage, while it's obvious that is the last thing I am likely to get from the Marquis!"

Eleta waited until Betty had slipped out to go to the bank and then she went to her father's room.

When her mother had married Cyril Warner, she had arranged for him to sleep in the room next to hers, but it was on the other side of the corridor.

This meant that her father's room remained very much his and his possessions were still there.

She entered the room and it somehow smelt musty and was just the same as it had been when she was a child, when she used to run in to talk to her father while he was dressing for dinner or getting ready to go riding.

What she was looking for and which she found at the back of a chest of drawers was a small revolver that he always carried when he went abroad.

"Is it dangerous where you go, Papa?" she recalled asking him.

"Sometimes," he replied. "But it's always best to be prepared for the worst. Therefore, because I carry what you would call a gun, I know I can protect myself however dangerous the enemy might be."

She remembered thinking at the time of her father shooting people instead of birds and she knew now that it was what she might want to do but for a different reason.

She found that the bullets were also in the drawer and took them and the revolver to her bedroom and put it right at the bottom of the case she was packing.

She had no wish to discuss the reason why she was taking it with Betty and then she began to pile on top of it the clothes she thought were most suitable for a Governess.

Fortunately those she had worn at school had been more or less plain, but she had no wish to leave behind all the pretty dresses she had bought in Paris, so she put them in another case.

She thought if she kept it locked, they would not be criticised by the Marquis's staff as being unsuitable for a Governess.

What was far more difficult was to pack her hats, as she could not bear to leave all the pretty ones behind.

She was thinking as she packed them that she might not stay long anyway with the obstreperous daughter of the Marquis. In which case she might have to go somewhere to find an entirely different position where her best dresses would be appreciated.

'I have to be practical about this,' she kept telling herself as she looked in the wardrobe.

Then she suddenly remembered that her mother had an enormous number of dresses of every sort and Eleta was certain that they had remained untouched since her death.

She went to her mother's room to find that she was not mistaken. The wardrobe was full, also the cupboards in the small dressing room opening out of the bedroom.

As she opened all the cupboard doors, there was a blaze of colour and the sweet scent of white violets.

Eleta was sure that it would please her Mama if she wore her dresses and, as she had always favoured rather classical designs, they were still in fashion.

Eleta took two of the prettiest and most elaborate of the evening gowns as well as a cape for travelling and a smart day dress she was sure her mother had never worn.

'One day perhaps I will need a great many more of them,' she mused.

Nothing could make her feel more protected than to be wearing her Mama's clothes and she had nearly finished packing when Betty came back from the bank.

"Here's the money, my Lady," she said, "and be extra careful it's not stolen from you."

"I will lock it away carefully, Betty, and the same with my jewel-case. I am not taking many jewels, for it would be a mistake for a Governess to appear in emeralds and diamonds!"

Betty laughed.

"It would indeed and, if you give your other jewels to me, I'll put them away in the safe in your mother's room and I have the only key."

Eleta thought this was a good idea, but at the same time she took with her the pearl necklace her father had given to her on her tenth birthday and a pair of earrings.

"You seem to have packed a great deal," Betty said, looking round the room. "I only hopes it means you'll stay there in peace and not come rushin' back after a week."

"I am not coming back," Eleta replied, "until my stepfather is convinced that he cannot succeed in making me marry the old Duke or until I am twenty-one and he no longer has any legal power over me."

Betty sighed.

"It may take just as long and, if you asks me, you'll soon be leavin' that terrible man's house and lookin' for somewhere quieter and safer."

"Well, do keep your eyes open in case something turns up where my stepfather would not find me, Make no mistake, I have no wish to be tied to anywhere, but as Papa once said, '*needs must when the Devil drives*'."

Betty put up her hands in horror.

"Don't say such things, my Lady, as they frighten me. So take care and, if it's difficult, come on home."

"To the Duke who might be waiting for me? It will have to be very very difficult before I do that."

She thought to herself that she had done her best, but she could not insist that Eleta should stay here under the present circumstances.

Tea had been brought upstairs to Eleta while she was packing, but she had been very careful not to let the footman realise what she was doing.

When he carried it in, she had deliberately taken a dress out of one of the cases and hung it up in the open door of the wardrobe and it looked quite obvious, without her saying anything, that she was unpacking.

"Mrs. Buxton hopes that you'll enjoy your tea, my Lady," the footman said, "and she wants to know if you'll be going down for dinner."

"I think, as I am so tired after my journey, I would rather have dinner in my room," Eleta said. "Is the Master dining in or out?"

It was what the servants called Cyril Warner and Eleta never heard it without feeling irritated that he should be Master in her mother's and father's house.

The footman hesitated.

"I thinks," he said, "the Master be waiting to hear if your Ladyship be dining upstairs or down."

Eleta thought this was good news, as it meant there were no guests and if she stayed upstairs her stepfather would probably go to his Club.

"Please ask Mrs. Buxton just to send me up a little soup and perhaps an omelette and tell the Master I have a bad headache and am going straight to bed."

"I'll tell them both, my Lady," the footman replied and disappeared.

Eleta then undressed and climbed into bed.

She was trying to think over as she did so of all the items she must take with her, just in case she did not return home for a long time.

At the same time she could not help feeling that she was leaving something very precious behind her.

It was all her feelings and thoughts for her mother whom she had always associated with this house.

It had never been a real home for her since her mother had married again. Yet it had always been there, as the house in the country had always been in her dreams.

She had imagined herself riding over the land she had ridden over when she was a child and swimming in the lake in front of the house.

It was all so large a part of her childhood and it seemed incredible that, now she was back in England, she could not go there and feel as she had felt when she was very young.

She remembered so vividly the first pony she had ridden and later the first horse.

No house – and she had visited a great number of them in many parts of the world – could ever be the same as the house in the country which was her real home.

On the way back from France she had been musing how exciting it would be to go there at the weekend.

Even if her stepfather had accompanied her, which she had hoped he would not do, she would still have felt the thrill of being home. Of running to the stables for the horse she wanted to ride, sliding down the banisters which she had done as soon as she was old enough to do so!

It was all part of her. The home she now could not go to, simply because if she stayed even one more day in London she would inevitably be confronted by the Duke.

'I must escape, I must,' she told herself again and again before she fell asleep.

*

It was Betty who wakened her when it was still dark, although the stars were not as bright as they had been earlier in the night.

"It's a quarter-past four, my Lady," Betty said, "and you should be out of the house in twenty minutes in case someone is up early."

In her mother's day the staff had been on duty at five o'clock and Eleta was suspicious that now many of them rose much later.

However, she knew that Betty was wise to take no risks and she must be out of the house before anyone could see her leaving.

She dressed quickly with Betty's help and she told her that she had taken the luggage after the servants had gone to bed and placed it on the staircase inside the door of the Agency.

"You are an angel, Betty," Eleta sighed. "Don't forget to give me back the key."

Eleta dressed in the same plain coat and skirt she had worn yesterday, but, as she thought it was chilly, she put on the cape she had taken from her mother's room.

Because it smelt of violets she reckoned that her Mama was standing guard over her and there would be no difficulty in getting away from London.

As she gazed round the room, she believed that she had remembered everything.

Betty was putting on her bonnet and black cape.

"You are coming with me!" Eleta exclaimed.

"Of course I am, my Lady. You don't suppose I'd let you walk the streets of London at night by yourself."

"I did not think of it, but, of course, Betty, I would love you to be with me. But I don't want you to get into trouble with Step-papa if he fancies I left the house and was accompanied by you."

"He won't know anythin' that you don't want him to know," Betty replied. "If I tells them in the kitchen, I've been to Church and am real astonished when your room is found empty, they'll believe me all right."

"You are a genius, Betty! You think of everything and I am so very grateful to you."

Eleta gave a deep sigh before she added,

"I have a feeling I would never have got away if you had not been here to help me."

"I'll be countin' the days until you comes back and you can be sure, my Lady, I'll let you know the moment the Master gives up the idea of your marryin' the Duke. But take care. If you're in any trouble with the Marquis, come back and we'll find somewhere else for you to hide."

"I know you will and thank you, darling Betty."

They crept down the back staircase and out through the door that led into the Square.

There was no one about, but it was not as dark as it had been and the first glimmer of light was just appearing over the roofs of the houses.

They walked quickly to the Agency to find that the road was deserted and everyone was still asleep.

"Now you stay quietly inside till the carriage comes for you," Betty said. "It's not likely you'll be disturbed at this time of the mornin', but as you know you can lock the door on the inside."

Eleta hugged Betty as she said goodbye to her and kissed her on both cheeks.

"You have been wonderful, wonderful," she said. "I will write to you, but I must disguise my writing in case any of the staff recognise it and tell Step-papa."

Betty nodded and Eleta went on,

"You can be quite certain he will be suspicious of everyone, especially of you, as you have always meant so much to me."

"I've thought of that," Betty said.

She opened her rather ugly handbag and pulled out a piece of paper.

"Here's the address of my sister-in-law, my Lady, and if you write to me there, she'll forward the letter on."

"How clever of you," Eleta exclaimed. "I did not think of that and, if I do write to you, it would not be surprising if your sister-in-law writes to you whenever she feels like it."

"That's what I want you to do. I'll tell her to put it in another envelope so that the Master won't be curious as to why I'm hearin' from Hertfordshire."

Eleta gave a cry of delight and kissed Betty again.

It would have been dark inside Mrs. Hill's house if there had not been a glass panel above the door and the dawn was just beginning to percolate through it.

Eleta sat on the stairs. It was not very comfortable, but at least she was resting her legs.

Then, as she was alone in the quiet of what was at the moment an empty house, she began to pray.

She prayed for God to help her and for her mother to be near her and she also prayed that where she was going would not be as difficult or as frightening as Betty feared it would be.

The sun was coming through the top of the door and lighting the stairs when Eleta's wristwatch told her that it was now six o'clock.

It was then that she turned the key in the lock and opened the door. Even as she did so, she saw a carriage approaching drawn by two horses.

When they were pulled in exactly outside the door, she opened it still further.

There was a footman on the box beside the driver and, as he came across the pavement, she saw that he was a comparatively young man with a smile on his lips.

"Be you the new Governess?" he enquired.

"I am," Eleta said, "and let me thank you for being so punctual."

"We was afraid we'd have difficulty findin' this place," he replied, "as we ain't been here before."

"My luggage is inside and thank you for coming."

"You may not thank me when you gets there," the footman muttered.

Eleta knew without being told what he meant and

she thought it would be a mistake to be too chatty. So she waited until the footman brought out her luggage and then she locked the door and put the key through the letter-box.

The footman loaded her luggage at the back of the carriage and then came round to open the door for her and she climbed inside.

It was very comfortable and well-upholstered and Eleta put her jewel-case down beside her, as the footman came to the door carrying her hat-box.

"Do you mind havin' this with you?" he asked. "It won't go into the hole at the back and I don't fancy havin' me legs on it all the way down."

"It will be quite all right on the small seat," Eleta said. "Or if you think it might fall, put it on the floor."

"If you asks me that's more sensible," the footman replied. "Do you want a rug over your knees, miss?"

"Thank you," Eleta said. "Now I am comfortable and I hope I will go to sleep."

"I could do with a wee bit of shut-eye meself," the footman said, "but there won't be no time for that."

He grinned as he closed the door and climbed up on the front seat and then they drove off.

The man was, she thought, somewhat cheeky for a footman and then she remembered she was no longer Lady Eleta Renton but just a Governess – someone he would say 'miss' to when he thought about it, but was more likely to forget it.

'Now that I am below stairs,' Eleta reflected, 'I will doubtless learn so much I did not know before.'

Yet, as she thought it over, she decided that she was not quite below stairs like the rest of the staff.

As one Governess had said to her years ago, her position was between Heaven and Hell!

She laughed at the time, but now she told herself it was no laughing matter and she would have to be careful to keep her dignity, while at the same time to be friendly and at ease with the other staff.

At least her stepfather would not expect her to be in such a position and she reckoned that he would first try to find her amongst her friends.

This would be much more difficult than it sounded because her friends of the last three years lived abroad and he would undoubtedly first ask her friends in France.

If he was at a loss as to where else she was likely to be, he only had to look at her letters to her mother.

The last batch of letters had been from Africa, but he would hardly expect her to travel all that way alone and before that there were letters she had written from Spain and Portugal.

'If Step-papa has to write to all those people,' Eleta thought, 'it will certainly take him a good long time. And he will be embarrassed at having to say he has lost me.'

She almost laughed at that idea, knowing it was something her stepfather would never admit.

But he would have to make some excuse for being anxious to get in touch with her immediately.

She had locked her bedroom door before she left, slipping the key back into the room by pushing it under the door and onto the carpet inside.

They would either have to break down the door to get in or find another key that fitted it.

She could imagine all too clearly her stepfather's fury and anger when he found her room empty and only a few clothes left in the wardrobe.

He would know then that she had gone away and there would be no one in the house to inform him when she left or where she went.

Eleta knew that she could trust Betty.

She would be surprised, astonished and appear very worried because she was not there, all of which would be of no help to her stepfather, who would be frantic in his efforts to find her.

'It will never enter his head for a moment,' Eleta thought, 'that I would go to an Agency and find a situation for which I was being paid.'

Seeing how rich she was, that would never occur to him, any more than he had expected her to run away.

If he had thought of it, she was certain he would have locked her in her bedroom and at night put a guard on the door without her being aware of it.

'I think I am safe, I am almost sure I am,' she told herself. 'But I must not take any chances. It is essential, if the Marquis entertains his friends, they do not see me.'

Then she told herself that was not as dangerous as it might be.

She had not been in England since her mother had died and she had deliberately stayed away, as she could not bear to go back to the house without her. Above all she had no wish to be with her stepfather.

'How could I have imagined for a moment that he would try to marry me to a man I have never seen,' she asked herself, 'who is old and prepared to sell his title to the highest bidder.'

She shuddered because the very idea shocked her.

The carriage continued gathering speed as it went out of London and it was then that Eleta began to think of the future rather than the past.

'Why,' she asked herself, 'does this child have such a dislike of her Governesses? Why do they say she is so impossible and un-teachable that they leave almost as soon as they arrive?'

Because she had learnt to reason things out at the Convent, she had been successful at all her lessons.

Not only had she used her brain, but her perception, her imagination and what she liked to call her *Third Eye* and now she applied them all to what was waiting ahead for her.

This passed the time far more quickly than anything else she could have done.

It was twelve o'clock before the carriage turned in at some large and majestic gold-topped gates and drove up a long drive with ancient oaks on either side.

They made Eleta think of her own country house in Northamptonshire.

When she had her first glimpse of the Marquis's house, she thought it was, without exception, the finest and most attractive house she had ever seen.

It was certainly extremely impressive and she was to learn later that it was considered the greatest success of the Adam Brothers.

They passed over a bridge into a huge courtyard with the sun shining on at least a hundred windows.

Eleta had seen many great houses when she had been abroad, especially the beautiful châteaux in France.

None, however, could equal the magnificence of Teringford Court, which excelled them all.

As they drew up at the front door, it flashed through her mind that, however short her stay might be, she must fully explore this magnificent and wonderful house before she left.

CHAPTER FOUR

An elderly butler bowed to Eleta.

"Good morning," she began somewhat shyly. "I am Miss Lawson, the new Governess."

He looked at her in surprise and she realised that he was thinking she was far too young, but he then said,

"If you'll come this way, miss, I'll take you to his Lordship's secretary, Mr. Clarke, who I know will want to see you."

There were two footmen in very smart livery in the hall and the butler led Eleta under the carved staircase and along a passage that she was sure ended in the kitchens.

Half way there, however, he stopped at a door and opening it he announced in an almost stentorian tone,

"Miss Lawson, the new Governess, sir."

Mr. Clarke, an elderly man, was looking a bit tired.

He rose from his desk and held out his hand.

"I was informed that you would be arriving today, Miss Lawson," he said, "but I did not expect you so soon."

"They were kind enough in London," Eleta replied, "to allow me to leave early."

"Will you sit down?" Mr. Clarke asked.

He indicated a chair in front of his desk and she sat down on it, sitting stiffly upright.

"I expect you have been told," he said, as he seated himself, "that we have a difficult problem here."

"Yes, Mrs. Hill told me about it and I hope that I will be more successful than the other Governesses."

"I hope so too. It is very bad for a child to have women popping in and out, but you must forgive me if I say that you look almost too young for such a position."

Eleta opened her handbag and handed him the two references she had shown to Mrs. Hill.

He took them from her and read them slowly and then he commented,

"These are certainly complimentary and I can only hope, Miss Lawson, that you will not give up too quickly. I think that the Governesses who preceded you left because they would not give it a fair chance."

"I will certainly do my best."

"I can only wish you the very best of luck," Mr. Clarke said. "And thank you for giving us at least a try."

Eleta realised that he was trying to be friendly and she smiled at him before she added,

"If my problems are too heavy for me, I will come and ask you how I can solve them. I have always thought a man is better at that than any woman."

Mr. Clarke laughed.

"I hope you are right and I certainly have a lot of problems to solve here as his Lordship is away so often."

Eleta felt in that case the Marquis was neglecting not only his estate but also his child.

She rose to her feet, saying,

"Will you be taking me up to meet my new pupil?"

Mr. Clarke shook his head.

"No, the housekeeper will do that. You will find that Mrs. Shepherd will show you round and of course will give you anything you require."

He touched the bell on his desk.

Immediately the door opened and an elderly woman in the traditional black of a housekeeper entered the room.

"Good morning, Mrs. Shepherd," Mr. Clarke said to her. "Allow me to introduce Miss Lawson, who has very kindly come as Governess to Lady Priscilla."

"That sounds a very long name for a very young girl," Eleta remarked.

"Her father used to call her 'Pepe'," Mr. Clarke answered, "but he is more formal now she is older."

Eleta did not reply, but, having shaken hands with Mrs. Shepherd, she said,

"As I have been travelling since very early this morning, you will understand I would like to go upstairs and take off my hat and cape."

"Of course Miss Lawson," the housekeeper agreed. "Your bedroom is in the nursery."

Eleta raised her eyebrows.

"So Lady Priscilla is still in the nursery," she asked, "even though she is old enough to have a Governess?"

The housekeeper looked surprised.

"We never thought of moving her, but if she wishes to have a larger room on a lower floor, there's no reason why she shouldn't, if that's what she wants."

"No one mentioned this to me," Mr. Clarke said as though they thought it might be his fault.

"Of course not, but it's something we must think about in the future."

Mrs. Shepherd gave a quick glance at Eleta, which told her quite clearly that she thought that she would not be staying long.

Eleta turned to Mr. Clarke,

"Thank you very much for being so kind and I hope I will not bother you too much."

"Of course, of course," Mr. Clarke replied quickly.

Mrs. Shepherd went the door and Eleta followed.

"I'm afraid that it's quite a long way upstairs," she said. "As you've just arrived, I think you should use the front stairs which I've always been told are very majestic."

"I should be delighted. As you can imagine, I am very impressed with this beautiful house."

"Everybody is. I only hope, Miss Lawson, that you stay here long enough to see all the treasures we have in practically every room."

They went up to the first floor and then climbed again to the second and Mrs. Shepherd stopped outside a white painted door.

Eleta was sure it was the nursery and suggested,

"I think, Mrs. Shepherd, after all I have heard of the difficulties that lie ahead, I would like to go in alone."

"You don't want me to introduce you to her?" Mrs. Shepherd asked in astonishment.

Eleta shook her head.

"If you don't think it rude of me, I would rather introduce myself."

"Well then, that's something new at any rate, but of course, Miss Lawson, you have your own way of doing things and we must respect them."

"Thank you, thank you very much, Mrs. Shepherd, and I expect if I am also to be sleeping in the nursery that my luggage will be brought up later."

She knew as she spoke from the expression on Mrs. Shepherd's face that she had not thought of a Governess being anywhere but in the nursery.

"I'll be in my room, which anyone'll show you to if you want me," Mrs. Shepherd said loftily.

Eleta then waited for Mrs. Shepherd to walk down the stairs and only when she had nearly reached the first floor did she open the door of the nursery and walk in.

The small occupant of it was sitting on the floor with a doll on her lap and a whole pile of tin soldiers and other small toys were scattered on the floor beside her.

She looked up when Eleta walked in, then sprang to her feet and stood at the window with her back to her.

Eleta closed the door behind her and, when she was halfway across the room, the child then turned and said,

"Go away! I am *not* doing any lessons! I hate – "

Before she could say any more, Eleta interrupted,

"Hush! Hush!"

She put her fingers to her lips and the child stared at her and she said again,

"Hush! Hush!"

Then, walking across the room, Eleta opened the door nearest the window.

She was right in thinking that it was the child's bedroom. It was a pretty room and well furnished.

Eleta looked in and then again she put her fingers to her lips before she said in a low whisper,

"We will not be heard in here. I have something to ask you."

Lady Priscilla was staring at her in amazement and, as she hesitated, Eleta whispered,

"They might be listening at the door."

She went to the bedroom, saying again quietly,

"Please come in."

Slowly and as if she could hardly believe what was happening, Lady Priscilla followed her and, when she was inside, Eleta breathed,

"Shut the door."

The child obeyed her and Eleta sat down on the bed and, pulling off her hat, she threw it behind her. She then loosened her cape and let it fall down around her.

Then she said again in a whisper,

"I want your help."

Lady Priscilla, from just inside the door, asked,

"*My* help?"

"Hush! I want to ask you something very secret."

Almost as if she was mesmerised by the way Eleta was behaving, Lady Priscilla moved towards the bed.

"I want your help," Eleta murmured again.

"My help?" the girl repeated, "but why?"

"I will tell you, but first I want you to promise to keep everything I tell you absolutely secret."

Lady Priscilla just stared at her, as Eleta went on,

"So secret that I can only beg of you to help me, please, please help me, I need it so much."

"I don't understand. How can I help you?"

"Come, sit down and I'll tell you why it's secret."

Lady Priscilla sat down at the end of the bed.

"If you will help me, I will be very very grateful. But, as I have just said, it is something very secret that no one must know except you."

"Why is what you are going to tell me so secret?"

"I will tell you why and then you will understand, but first you must promise me on your honour that you will tell no one what I am going to tell you."

"I promise."

"Then cross your heart like this," Eleta said, and she crossed her own heart with her first finger.

Rather slowly, because she had not done it before, Lady Priscilla followed her.

"Now you have promised me, I will tell you the truth, which you will understand is so very secret."

"What is it?" Lady Priscilla asked.

"I have run away," Eleta whispered.

"Run away! But why?"

"My father and mother are dead and my horrible stepfather wants me to marry an old man simply because he is important and will help him in with his business."

She spoke slowly so that Lady Priscilla would not miss a word and after a moment the child enquired,

"So you ran away and they don't know where you have gone."

"That is true and it is very clever of you to realise it, but if they find out where I am, I will have to go back and marry this terrible old man."

"So you want to stay here?" Lady Priscilla muttered as if she was working it out in her mind.

"I would like to stay here," Eleta said, "but I am not really a Governess, I never have been one and, if they find out that about me, I will be sent away at once."

She drew in her breath before she added,

"Please, please help me. Only you can help me by pretending I am a Governess."

"How can I pretend?"

"I was thinking about that as I was coming down from London. As I cannot teach you anything, you will have to pretend you are learning from me."

"How can I do that?" Lady Priscilla asked.

"The first thing I thought of was that everyone who comes to this house says how magnificent it is."

Lady Priscilla nodded.

"Then you will say that you always think the Adam Brothers designed wonderful houses."

She saw that the child looked surprised and added,

"That is all you have to say and they will think how clever you are."

"What else will I have to say?"

"We will have to pretend we are doing lessons," Eleta answered. "And we will think of things which will make people believe that you are learning a lot."

"What sort of things will I have to say?"

"For instance when your father is here and you see him early in the morning you say, '*bonjour, mon père,*' just three words, but he will think you are learning French."

Lady Priscilla laughed.

"That's very funny," she giggled.

"We will think up lots of ideas to impress people and they will be sure I am a very very good Governess."

"You said we have to pretend to have lessons?"

"We will write something in notebooks," Eleta said casually. "When they look at them, they will think we are having a long lesson on places I will tell you about. I have been to Paris and I have lovely stories about Egypt and also Greece, where I saw statues of the Gods and Goddesses."

"You will tell me about them?"

"Of course I will tell you stories. That is the best way we can pretend to be having lessons."

Lady Priscilla clapped her hands together.

"That sounds a very different kind of lesson from what the other Governesses wanted me to do."

"I told you I am not a Governess," Eleta replied, "so you will have to tell me how I should behave like one."

Lady Priscilla giggled again.

"That will be funny, *me* teaching *you*!"

"If you are going to help me, that is what you will have to do. If I am sent away, I have nowhere else to go. Then if I go back to my stepfather, I will have to marry that horrid old man."

"I will not let them send you away," Lady Priscilla asserted. "But what shall we do?"

"I can see that there is so much to do here," Eleta replied. "I am sure there are many wonderful horses in the stables and we will ride and ride so that no one will ever know where we are or can listen to what we say."

"You can ride!" Lady Priscilla exclaimed. "None of my other Governesses wanted to ride."

"Well I want to ride," Eleta said. "I love riding and we will ride for miles and miles so that no one can snatch me up and take me back to London."

"I will stop them from doing that!"

"If you are really going to help me," Eleta said, "I can only say thank you, thank you from the bottom of my heart. I was so frightened you would send me away and I would have to go back to my wicked stepfather."

"I will not send you away and I am sure if they think I am having lessons no one will want you to go."

"Then we must act our parts very cleverly. I have to pretend I am a Governess, but really you will be teaching me what I have to do. And I will just tell you what you have to say so that no one is suspicious."

"We must stop them, of course we will stop them."

"Thank you, thank you," Eleta exclaimed. "I was so frightened I would be sent straight back to London and my stepfather would be waiting for me."

"You must stay here," Lady Priscilla said firmly, "and I will be very careful to say that you are teaching me lots and lots of things I don't know."

"That will be true anyway. I hate telling lies and I am going to tell you stories about all the exciting places I have been to and I am sure there are endless stories hidden in this house that no one else has ever found."

Lady Priscilla's eyes were shining.

"About what? Can you tell me a story?"

"Well, show me your picture gallery and I will tell you stories about the paintings. I have seen a great many pictures in Paris, in Rome and also in Spain."

Eleta paused for a moment and then she said,

"I expect you have a big library."

"It's full of books and I hate books," Lady Priscilla pouted.

"But the stories are always good in the best books," Eleta told her. "So I will read them and then tell you the story afterwards in my own words."

"That will be fun," Lady Priscilla answered.

There was a knock on the door outside the nursery.

"What is that?" Eleta asked.

"I expect it's luncheon. You must be hungry after coming all the way from London."

"I am, now I think about it," Eleta replied. "But I was so frightened you would send me away that I could not think of anything else.

"Of course I am not going to send you away."

"Then be careful what you say in front of anyone," Eleta whispered. "The walls have ears and always hear what you don't want them to hear."

Lady Priscilla laughed as if she thought it funny and then she peeped outside the door and turned to say,

"Yes, it is luncheon and it's on the table."

"Let's eat quickly and then perhaps you can take me to the stables. I am sure that you have superb horses here and, as I told you, I love horses."

"Shall we go riding?" Lady Priscilla asked.

She spoke as if she thought it very unlikely and Eleta was sure that she loved riding just as she herself had loved it at her age.

"Do you think, do you really think we can?"

"Of course we can," Lady Priscilla replied.

"You can say you want to show me the woods and I have a riding habit in my luggage."

"Then we can go riding. So I will tell Harry, the footman, who is bringing in the luncheon."

Eleta rose from the bed and tidied away her hat and then, as she went into the nursery, she heard Harry say,

"Yes, my Lady. I'll tell them to have your pony ready for you and a horse for the Governess."

As Harry closed the door, Eleta walked in from the bedroom.

She could see the food was laid out on the table, but as she had expected it was plain nursery food and, although she made no comment, she was thinking it would be much more sensible if Lady Priscilla had her meals downstairs.

However, she did not say anything but helped Lady Priscilla and herself to the rather wishy-washy dishes.

They would be suitable, she thought, for a child much younger and were very unsuitable, as far as she was concerned, for a Governess.

Because she hoped it would be interesting, she told the child about the horses she had ridden and how she had loved them.

"When I left England and went to school," she said, "I cried, not because I was going abroad, but because I was leaving the horses I loved and which I know loved me."

She saw that Lady Priscilla was interested and then told her the horses' names and how she had ridden round the Racecourse and had managed to clear all the jumps.

"I want to do that!" Lady Priscilla exclaimed.

"Of course you do, but I expect your pony is getting too small for you."

"Much too small for me and I am not allowed to ride without a leading rein."

"Do you ride well?" Eleta asked her.

"Very very well, but they still make me go with a leading rein, although I know I am quite safe without one."

"Of course you are," Eleta agreed. "We will not tell them, but we will take it off as soon as we get away from the stables."

She saw the excitement in Lady Priscilla's eyes and she knew that this was another reason that had made the child angry and difficult.

Half-an-hour later they rode out of the stables after the Head Groom had handed Eleta the leading rein.

She had already had to struggle with him when he offered her a horse she considered was almost an insult and she had some difficulty in persuading him to saddle up the horse she wanted.

As soon as they were out of sight of the stables, Eleta then took the leading rein from Lady Priscilla, who unfastened it from her pony's bridle.

"Now we can go really fast," she cried.

"I want to see first how well you can ride and then I am going to ask for a far larger pony or even a horse, if I think you can manage it," Eleta told her.

There was no doubt that the child took after her father and was in fact an excellent rider.

They galloped across the nearest field and turned into a wood.

"I really love woods," Eleta said. "They are always exciting and I am quite certain that there are real goblins under the ground and fairies among the leaves."

"The Governess before you told me there were no such things as fairies and goblins were imaginary creatures who don't really exist."

"Of course they exist, but only people like you and me who believe in them ever see them. I am quite certain I have seen goblins in the wood at home and I am sure that they are working here underground."

Lady Priscilla gave a gasp and Eleta went on,

"As for fairies, we will find a circle of mushrooms where they have danced the night before and then we will be quite certain there are plenty of them here as well as in the garden with the lovely flowers."

"Do tell me more!" Lady Priscilla begged.

"I think we should keep the stories for this evening when we have nothing else to do," Eleta suggested. "Now I want to gallop very very fast towards that hill I can see in the distance."

"That hill has a big cave at the very top of it," Lady Priscilla said. "No one will ever let me go near it."

"Why not?" Eleta asked.

"Because they say it's dangerous and there are lots of other caves inside it, so I might get lost."

"That sounds very thrilling and something we must explore one day," Eleta said.

She knew that the child was delighted at the idea and then, as they were riding home, Eleta said,

"I cannot go on calling you Lady Priscilla, it is such a long name. I would like to call you Pepe, which I think your father called you when you were quite small?"

"He sometimes does now," she replied. "But he is usually so angry with me for sending away a Governess, that when he is here I get a long lecture."

"Please don't send me away," Eleta begged, "then he will not be able to lecture you."

"I don't want you to go away, you tell me the most marvellous stories."

"I haven't started yet, but I promise you there are hundreds and hundreds of stories in the house alone."

As they rode back, she was thinking it was without exception the finest house she had ever seen.

"It must be full of stories," she said aloud, "and, when you take me round to explore it – and I would much rather *you* did than be taken by Mrs. Shepherd, I know we will find a story in every room, perhaps two or three."

"How will you find them?" Pepe asked.

Eleta thought for a moment and then she said,

"I think, maybe, when there is a marvellous story hidden in a room either in a book or because something has happened here in the past, if we are clever it will come into our minds."

"And if it comes into your mind, will you tell me?"

"Yes, but if it goes into your mind first you will have to tell it to me."

Pepe laughed.

"We will be telling each other stories all the time."

"Of course, and why not?" Eleta asked. "They are far more interesting than conversation and some stories are very exciting."

"And you will tell them all to me?"

"Yes, I will and it will be a very special lesson."

"It seems a funny lesson compared to the sort the others tried to give me," Pepe sighed.

"But I am a very funny sort of Governess. As you know, you are helping me and saving me and therefore I am the heroine. You must be writing a book in your mind whenever you think about me."

Pepe was thrilled at this idea, so thrilled that, when they neared the house, Eleta said,

"We must not forget the wonderful stories we are going to find and if we make notes about them we will not forget them. One day, Pepe, you will write them down and they will be published and you will be a famous author."

"But I really *hate* books," Pepe said, as if the word automatically came to her lips.

"There are books and books," Eleta replied, "just as there are people and people. Some people we love, who are very wonderful, and it would be lovely to write about them, but some people are wicked and horrid and we must just forget them."

She saw that the child was thinking over what she had just said and finally she replied,

"If they are wicked, they are the villains!"

"Yes, of course they are, Pepe, but you and I are the heroines and the good people who will always be helped not only by the fairies but by the angels."

This started a new train of thought and they were still talking about angels and whether there was one for everyone in Heaven when they reached the stables.

"I see her Ladyship's ridin' without a leadin' rein," the Head Groom said. "I don't know what his Lordship'll say about that."

"Her Ladyship is quite old enough and competent to ride on her own," Eleta said, "But she should have a larger pony or even a horse. She really rides very well."

"I don't know what his Lordship'll think about it. We've always bin extra careful about her Ladyship and there'll be terrible trouble if she has an accident."

"I promise you she is not going to have one," Eleta said. "I am sure because you are so clever you will find a larger pony or a horse for her to ride tomorrow."

She realised in flattering him that she had said the right thing, as after a moment's pause he replied,

"I'll do me best, but I might not be able to find one as quickly as that."

Eleta smiled, thanked him and, as they went into the house, she suggested,

"I think it would be nice if we had tea downstairs, if not in the drawing room, there must be other comfortable rooms where we can sit in beautiful surroundings, which, of course, make wonderful stories for us."

"I would love to do that," Pepe enthused, "but they always say I have to stay in the schoolroom, which, as you know, is really my nursery."

"I do realise that and, as there is no one else in the house, I am now going to ask the butler to bring us tea in whichever room you fancy best for our stories."

"The tapestry room has stories on the tapestries, but no one would tell me what they are all about."

"Very well, Pepe, we will have tea in the tapestry room today. Then tomorrow we will find another room where there will also be stories but different ones."

They walked in through the front door and there was no butler to be seen, only two footmen on duty.

"Lady Priscilla and I would like tea in the tapestry room," Eleta said. "We are now going upstairs to change, but we will not be long."

The footmen looked at her in astonishment.

"In the tapestry room?" one of them queried. "But her Ladyship always has her tea upstairs."

Eleta smiled.

"She is too old for the nursery now and I hope we will find a more comfortable schoolroom, so when we have finished tea I would then like to see Mrs. Shepherd."

She spoke politely, but with an authority that the footman readily acknowledged.

"Very well, miss," he said.

"I will race you up the stairs," Eleta suggested.

Pepe gave a cry of excitement and they both started to run and Eleta allowed the child to win by just one stair.

They were both laughing as they climbed the next staircase hand in hand.

"Now hurry and change," Eleta urged.

A housemaid appeared from nowhere and it was clearly her job to help Pepe to dress and undress.

Eleta then went into her room next door, which she thought was very ordinary and rather dreary. Only one of her boxes had been unpacked as the others were locked.

Then, throwing her riding clothes onto a chair, she put on a pretty but comfortable dress.

Then she and Pepe went downstairs.

The tapestry room was obviously very special and it was indeed one of the finest Eleta had ever seen and the tapestries themselves were varied, but they all had pictures woven into them.

She made up a story for the first one and Pepe for the second and the way she spoke told Eleta that she was not only intelligent but imaginative.

It was a pity that she had not been encouraged to use both in the past rather than try to force her to learn the humdrum lessons considered necessary for all children.

When they had finished tea, Eleta proposed,

"As we have done a lot already, I think it would be a mistake to visit the picture gallery today, because there are so many stories there for us to tell each other later on."

She thought that the child agreed and she added,

"I would like you to take me to the music room. I am sure you have one here in this lovely house."

"We have a very big music room," Pepe said. "But the Governesses I have had could not play the piano and the teacher who came from the village gave up after I had only had three lessons."

"Why did she do that?" Eleta asked.

"Because I would not play the way she wanted me to," Pepe replied.

"I can show you how I would like you to play."

They walked a long way down a corridor and the music room was at the far end of it.

It was not only hung with fascinating pictures, but there were many plants coming into flower placed round the platform where there was a grand piano.

Eleta thought it was one of the finest she had seen anywhere.

She had forgotten for a moment that Pepe was with her, as she sat at the piano and played a piece that had been written by a Master not only of music but of romance.

Pepe listened spellbound and Eleta said,

"This is the most perfect piano to play on. And, of course, you must learn some lovely music. Sit down now and try it for yourself."

Pepe did so without argument.

She picked out the notes in some instinctive way and they all seemed to follow each other almost as if they were a real tune.

"I know one thing about you, if nothing else, Pepe."

"What is that?" she asked.

"One day you are going to be a real musician and the piano will inspire you. You will be writing tunes you hear in your mind that will be published."

"I hear tunes in my mind sometimes when I am in bed, but I could not play them on a piano."

"It is something you will do, Pepe, but you will have to do some practising first and I will play for you to show you how to do it."

"Please play for me again."

Eleta was only too willing and she played one tune after another until she realised that it was getting late and it was time for the child to have supper and go to bed.

"Now don't say a word," she said. "I am going to talk to Mrs. Shepherd and see if we can be moved down to prettier bedrooms and more comfortable ones."

Pepe looked excited.

"I am sure one of them," Eleta went on, "and there must be a great many in the house, must have a boudoir attached, which is far nicer than this rather dull nursery."

"That will be lovely. I want to be downstairs. I hate being up here in this old nursery. But they said this was to be my schoolroom."

"So we will just have to find something different," Eleta replied. "I think we would be wise if we talked first to Mr. Clarke."

"I like him," Pepe said unexpectedly. "He is a nice man and, when I told him once I had thrown a book out of the window, he laughed and said if it was very dull he would have wanted to do that himself at my age!"

Eleta laughed.

"Then I think he is just the person we want at the moment. Come along, we will go and see him before you have supper."

They walked to the office where Eleta had been that morning and Mr. Clarke was rather startled to see them.

When they told him that they had to talk to him, he sat down and was prepared to listen attentively.

"Now what we have decided," Eleta began, "is that Lady Priscilla is too old to be up in the nursery."

Mr. Clarke looked surprised and she continued,

"What we would like and we have discussed it very carefully is one of the bedrooms on the first floor that I am sure has a nice boudoir attached to it.

"If Lady Priscilla has a bedroom with an adjoining boudoir, it would be convenient if I could have a bedroom on the other side of the boudoir. Surely in a big house like this that is possible."

"Yes, of course it is," Mr. Clarke replied. "I am only surprised that you thought of it. It is something that has never occurred either to me or to Mrs. Shepherd."

"As I am sure all the rooms are ready for any guests who might happen to come," Eleta added, "we would like to move in immediately. As you can imagine I have no wish to unpack and then have to pack up again."

"I think by that statement you are contemplating staying with us," Mr. Clarke smiled.

Eleta looked at Pepe.

"It depends on Lady Priscilla," she said. "I do hope she will want me to stay."

"Of course I want you to stay and she is quite right, Mr. Clarke, in saying that I am too old for the nursery. I want a very pretty room and I would like a piano in it too."

"Now that's a really clever idea," Eleta said, "and something I did not think of myself. Of course you need a piano. You can practise at any odd moment and then go to the music room and play on that glorious piano without feeling it is laughing at us."

"I'm sure it would not laugh at you."

"I am not certain," Eleta said, "because I am rather out of practice. We will practise upstairs, you and I, and then go to the music room which will have to applaud us!"

Pepe laughed loudly and Eleta could see that Mr. Clarke's eyes were twinkling.

"I think," he said, "you would both be satisfied, which naturally is most important, if I gave you the King's room – named after George IV, who was supposed to have stayed here soon after he was made King."

Eleta gave a little cry.

"Oh, how brilliant! I do love reading about George IV and I know Lady Priscilla will adore the stories about him and all his bucks and beaux."

"I think a great number of them have been here at one time or another," Mr. Clarke said with a smile. "He was very dashing as the Prince of Wales and even more so as the Prince Regent."

Eleta knew that he was thinking of his many love affairs and also of his extravagance in what he spent on Carlton House and she was sure she could relate amusing stories about him for Pepe.

"I will tell Mrs. Shepherd to move all your things down there while you are having supper," Mr. Clarke said.

"That is very kind of you. They will have to hurry because, as we have so much to do tomorrow, I don't want Lady Priscilla to be overtired tonight."

"There are plenty of housemaids in the house to do things quickly if you require it," Mr. Clarke suggested.

He rang the bell on his desk sharply and the door was opened almost immediately by a footman.

"Ask Mrs. Shepherd to come here at once," he said, "and I also require three or four men like yourself,"

"Very good, sir," the footman replied.

Eleta rose to her feet.

"While they are moving us, I am just going back to the music room to play one last tune for Lady Priscilla. It will bring her new dreams tonight in her new bed and I think I shall be dreaming too."

"I know I will too," Mr. Clarke grinned. "I had no idea that anyone like you really existed."

"I often think that myself," Eleta replied and they both laughed.

Holding Pepe by the hand, she ran down the long corridor that led to the music room.

"Now close your eyes," Eleta said, "and see what story the music tells you and if you can see pictures of what is happening."

"I will do that," Pepe replied, sitting down on the nearest sofa.

Eleta went to the piano and played some of the soft romantic tunes she had danced to in Paris and those she had listened to at different theatres all over Europe.

She felt moved herself by them and was certain that the child would be too.

She was very still with her eyes closed and then, when Eleta stopped playing, she jumped up and went to the platform to stand beside her.

"That was wonderful and I have a lovely, lovely story to tell you!"

"And I have one to tell you too."

Eleta glanced at the door and said in a whisper,

"Thank you, thank you for helping me. You have been superb. I don't think they will send me away now."

"Send you away? I will scream and scream if they try to! And if they insist, I will come with you!"

"I think we will just stay here and enjoy ourselves."

Eleta bent and kissed Pepe on the cheek.

As if she knew instinctively what she was about to do, the child put her arms round her neck and hugged her.

"Now I'm going to tell you my story," she said "and it's a very exciting one."

CHAPTER FIVE

Eleta slept peacefully in the large canopied bed that reminded her of her own home.

She now felt more at ease than she had been since coming home from Paris.

Apparently Pepe slept very well too and they met for breakfast in the boudoir.

Eleta thought that it was a child's breakfast rather than a grown-up's.

As they finished, Pepe asked,

"Are we going riding?"

She had on her riding habit and so had Eleta, but for the moment Eleta paused before she replied,

"We have one thing to do first and I do want you to come with me and help me. We are going to see the cook."

"The cook!" Pepe exclaimed. "I am not allowed in the kitchen."

"You will be allowed if you are with me. I am sure you agree that we need more exciting food than this."

She did not wait for an answer, but walked towards the door and Pepe came running after her.

They went down the stairs and, when they reached the hall, Eleta said to the nearest footman,

"I want to see the cook. Will you find out if she is available?"

He looked at her in surprise and replied,

"She's a he!"

"A man?" Eleta questioned.

"Yes, his name is Monsieur Téyson."

Eleta's eyes lit up, but she said nothing. She just took hold of Pepe's hand and followed the footman.

They passed the pantry and she had a brief glimpse of the safe and then there was a door that obviously led into the kitchen.

"Here you are," the footman said. "I expects you'll find him there all right."

She walked into the kitchen and saw an elderly man working at the large table in the centre and one look told her that he was a Frenchman.

She therefore began,

"*Bonjour, monsieur.*"

The chef looked up in surprise and answered,

"*Bonjour, mademoiselle.*"

Then, looking at Pepe, he said,

"Good morning, my Lady."

Then Eleta, in her best Parisian French, started to talk to him.

She told him who she was and that she was very anxious for her Ladyship to learn French and what could be better than if she first learnt the names of French dishes.

"The French are the best cooks in the world," she said. "I have travelled a great deal, but I have never found anything as good as French *cuisine.*"

The chef was at first astonished at her addressing him in such excellent French and then his eyes twinkled.

He knew without being told, Eleta thought, that she was making her pupil interested in French, but in a very different way from any of her other Governesses.

Finally he said,

"Of course, *mademoiselle*, you are right. We will teach French through mouth, taste and stomach and result will be *fantastique!*"

"I thought you would understand and I am most grateful to you. I know that his Lordship will be pleased if his daughter learns languages and naturally nothing is more important in Europe than French."

The chef was delighted at the compliment.

"I have something for the young lady, some *petits fours* I believe she like"

He turned and Eleta whispered to Pepe,

"When he gives you his *petits fours* say, '*merci bien, monsieur*'."

She then repeated the words twice, so that she was certain that Pepe understood.

The chef came back with a box of *petits fours* that Eleta knew at a glance would be delicious.

He arranged several of them on a plate and then he handed them to Pepe.

"*Merci – bien – monsieur*," she said slowly.

The chef was astonished and clapped his hands.

"*Vous parlez Francais!*" he exclaimed. "That very good, his Lordship be delighted."

"I am sure he will," Eleta agreed.

Pepe was eating his *petits fours* and said that they were delicious, as Eleta expected.

"Now Monsieur Téyson," Eleta said, "is going to give us French food and you must learn the names of every dish, so that you can ask for it again."

"These are really, really scrummy," Pepe enthused, "I would like to have these every day."

"Then ask Monsieur to make them for you again. If you thank him once more in French he will not forget."

"*Merci bien, monsieur*," she repeated obediently.

The chef clapped his hands again with delight.

As they turned away to leave the kitchen, Eleta was aware that the butler was standing in the doorway and that he had been listened to them.

"I am sure you will agree with me," Eleta said to him, "that Monsieur's brilliant dishes must not get cold going up to the first floor. I therefore think in future that her Ladyship and I should eat in the dining room, both for luncheon and for supper."

The butler stared at her and Eleta thought for a moment that he was going to argue and then he said,

"I'll arrange that, miss."

Eleta felt that she had gained a victory and then she hurried Pepe out to the stables.

The Head Groom had a horse for her that was not too large and he said it was perfectly broken in so that she would not find it difficult to ride.

Eleta thanked him and Pepe was delighted.

"Now I can ride really fast like you," she smiled.

"But first you have to talk to your new horse and make him realise that you are in charge of him and he must do what you tell him."

"Talk to him! Will he understand?"

"Of course he will. My father always made me talk to my horses before I could ride them. They recognised the sound of my voice and knew just what I required them to do. But first we must find out the name of your horse."

"He be called Silver Star," the Head Groom said.

"What a lovely name!" Pepe exclaimed, "and thank you for finding me such a beautiful horse."

She held out her arms to Silver Star and then talked to him very quietly.

She was rather shy of being overheard and then to encourage her Eleta drew the Head Groom away to ask his advice about one of the other horses.

She did not, however, leave Pepe for long and very shortly they were riding off into the paddock.

The child was thrilled with her new mount and Eleta was aware that she was handling the horse extremely well and would come to no harm.

They rode off over the fields and through the wood and, when Pepe wanted to go up to the top of the hill that towered over the field, Eleta shook her head.

"We will explore it another day. I have to find out if it is really dangerous as you have been told it is or if that was an excuse to stop you climbing up on your own."

Pepe laughed.

"I think the Governesses I had before you were so old they did not want to walk so far."

"Well, we will find out why you were told not to go there, but now, as it is nearly luncheontime, I suggest we go back through the woods and look for the goblins. Then afterwards we will go down to the lake and have a swim."

Pepe looked at her in astonishment.

"Go for a swim! Can we really go into the water?"

"Yes, we can, have you not been there before?"

"I went swimming in the sea two years ago, but I kept being bowled over by the waves. Papa swims in the lake, but the Governesses would not let me swim too."

"Well, I love swimming," Eleta volunteered, "and that is what we will do this afternoon."

*

It was what they were to do almost every afternoon for the next two weeks and by then Pepe was beginning to swim quite well.

Eleta loved the swimming and enjoyed it almost as much as riding the splendid horses in the stables.

She had difficulty in persuading the Head Groom to let her try out a different horse every day, but, when he saw how well she rode, he let her choose the one she fancied.

She also found that there was a hut near the part of the lake where they swam and she then persuaded the Head Gardener to move it nearer to the water.

They could undress there and dress again instead of going back to the house in wet bathing suits and she asked for fresh towels to be put in the hut every day.

Eleta felt that she had made Pepe's life far more comfortable at Teringford Court than it had been.

*

On the tenth day of her visit Eleta had only just gone to bed when there was a huge crash in the sky and she realised that rain was pouring through her open window.

She jumped out of bed and ran to shut the window and there were more crashes and flashes outside.

It was then a little voice from the door that led into the boudoir murmured,

"I am – frightened."

Eleta closed the window and answered,

"So am I, Pepe. Jump into my bed and we will be frightened together."

Pepe ran across the room and slipped into the bed.

Eleta joined her and, as soon as she came in next to her, Pepe moved towards her, hiding her face against her shoulder.

Eleta's arms went round her.

"Don't be frightened, Pepe. It's only the naughty clouds fighting each other in the sky. They are like little boys and later the sun comes out and it is all forgotten."

"It frightens me – because it's so noisy," the child whispered. "But I am safe here with you."

Eleta's arms tightened.

"Absolutely safe. We must not be afraid because soon everything will be beautiful and quiet again."

"That sounds like a story – "

Eleta laughed.

"In other words you are asking me to tell you one."

"Yes, please."

Pepe moved a little closer and Eleta soothed her,

"You know that you ought to go to sleep. There is so much to do tomorrow, so I will just tell you a very short story about the angels looking after us."

"I'd like that."

"I am sure," Eleta began, "that your angel is just like you only she would not have such a long name."

"Then what is my angel called?" the child asked.

"She is called 'Pepe', which your father called you when you were small and what I have been calling you."

"If my angel has a pretty name which is also mine, what is yours called?"

Eleta hesitated for a moment and then she replied,

"My real name is of course secret. If I tell you, you must be very careful to call me by it only when no one is listening, in case they talk and my stepfather finds me."

"I will be very very careful," she promised.

"Then it is 'Eleta'."

"Oh, that's a pretty name. So much prettier than saying 'Miss Lawson'."

"That is a pretend name, but you must remember to use it in front of the servants and anyone else in the house."

She thought it extraordinary that apparently so few people called at Teringford Court and they had not heard anything from the Marquis since she had arrived here.

"I will be very careful that no one shall take you away from me," Pepe was saying.

"You know I want to stay with you."

"Do you really and truly want to, Eleta?"

"I love being here," Eleta replied, "and I love being with you. In fact, Pepe, I love you very much."

Pepe moved a little closer.

"And I love you too," she sighed. "I do love you, Eleta, and you must never, never leave me."

"I will try not to and I am very grateful to you for being so kind to me."

"I love you, I love you," Pepe repeated.

Eleta kissed her and she stayed in her arms until she fell asleep.

*

The next morning, when they went downstairs to breakfast, the butler brought in a delicious dish of salmon cooked as only a Frenchman could do it.

"His Lordship's coming home today," he said.

Eleta stared at him, thinking that she could not have heard right.

"His Lordship?" she repeated.

The butler nodded.

"They sent a runner, as we call them, from London to say His Lordship'll be coming back alone and there's to be no guests this weekend."

Pepe gave a little cry,

"I hope Papa will not send us back to the nursery!"

"I am sure he will not do that," Eleta replied.

At the same time she felt anxious and worried and the Marquis might upset Pepe and make her as difficult as she had apparently been with him on his other visits.

"There was a long piece about his Lordship in the newspaper yesterday," the butler was now saying. "I don't know whether you saw it, Miss Lawson, but it says a great deal about this house and the treasures in it."

"I didn't read the newspapers yesterday because we were so busy. But I do hope, if the house has been written about in the newspaper, that we will not attract burglars."

"Not much fear of that," the butler replied. "We have two nightwatchmen in the house and there be a man in the stables and another in the garden during the night."

"I had no idea, but makes me feel safe."

"His Lordship's seen to it and there's enough locks and bolts on the house to keep an army at bay."

When they were alone, she said to Pepe,

"I wonder what time your father will arrive?"

"He usually comes in the afternoon. Then he hears how cross the Governess is and he gives me a lecture."

"Well, this time he will have a surprise," Eleta said. "We must think how we can astound him with everything you can now do that he has never seen or heard before."

Pepe thought that this was a good idea.

"We'll give him such a surprise that he will want you to stay here for ever and ever, which is what I want."

"First you must show how pleased you are to see him. You run to him and say, 'Daddy, Daddy, I am so glad to have you back' and then you give him a big kiss."

"I don't usually call him 'Daddy'."

"It sounds more cosy and loving than 'Papa' and we have to make him realise that you are very different from the little girl he last saw."

"Do I look very different?" Pepe asked.

"You do and I know you are happy, just as I am."

"Of course I am so happy when you tell me those wonderful stories and I am learning to play the piano."

"You also ride a big horse that your father has not seen and I am sure he will be proud of you."

"He may be angry and say I have to go back to my pony and be led on a leading rein," Pepe replied.

"I am sure you will not have to do that."

She thought unless the Marquis was blind, deaf and dumb, he could not help being astonished by the difference in his daughter.

Eleta was quite convinced now on one thing.

It was that Pepe was musical and in a very short time she would be able to play the piano far better than most girls of her age and it went without saying that she had inherited her father's way with horses.

She would, when she was older, be an outstanding rider, but the most important difference was that she was now a happy child.

She was thrilled with everything they did together and then used her brain to put forward new ideas and new interests that had never been developed before.

What was more, no one could help loving her.

"Now we must play our game carefully, Pepe. If you think that your father will arrive about teatime or later,

I think we should go riding this morning and then have a swim before luncheon."

"Yes, let's do that," Pepe agreed. "It will be very exciting for me and I will surprise Papa by showing him how well I can swim."

"We will show him that tomorrow," Eleta said. "I think this afternoon we might stay in the music room for a while and then perhaps go and see if there are any new flowers out in the garden."

She was anxious that Pepe should be well-dressed and looking pretty when her father returned and so it would be a mistake to be too active after luncheon.

They went for a ride taking the horses rather slower than usual because it was so hot.

When they returned to the house, they then hurried down to the lake.

They quickly took off their clothes in the hut and put on their bathing dresses which were dry and clean.

Pepe wore a cap over her hair, while Eleta pinned her fair curly hair on top of her head – it was so long that it hung when it was loose over her breasts, but she managed to keep it out of the water.

Pepe plunged into the lake. She had been able to swim only a little when Eleta arrived, but now it came to her naturally and she swam about as if she was a little fish.

Eleta was glad that she had been sensible enough to pack a very attractive bathing dress. She had bought it in France for when she stayed with one of her friends.

It was the pale blue of her eyes and had, which the French had introduced, a short skirt from the waist nearly to her knees. It made her look very young and was also extremely becoming.

She had a perfect figure and had caused a sensation when she appeared in it in France. The men present had complimented her on being a Goddess of the Sea.

But there was no one to see her now except Pepe and it was glorious swimming in the cool water with the sun reflected on it.

Eleta was just thinking that it was time for them to go back to the house for luncheon when a man appeared, walking over the lawn.

For a moment she wondered who he was.

Then Pepe, who had gone into the hut to take off her bathing dress, came out of the door in her petticoat.

She was just about to say something to Eleta when she saw the man coming down to the water's edge.

For a moment she stared at him and then she gave a cry and ran towards him calling out,

"Daddy, Daddy, you are back! It's so lovely to see you!"

As she reached the Marquis, he put out his hands and picked her up.

To his surprise she put her arms around his neck, hugging him and kissing his cheek.

*

The Marquis had quite suddenly, as he often did, decided that London was boring and he wanted to be in the country.

It was not only the heat but the fact that he had attended a large number of parties in the last few weeks.

He had also decided that his *affaire-de-coeur* with the beautiful Countess of Westbridge was at an end as far as he was concerned.

It was not that she was not as beautiful as she had been when he had first seen her or that she was in any way difficult or over-demanding.

It was just because he found, as he inevitably did in all his affairs, that she had nothing new to offer him and he anticipated what she was about to say before she said it.

'It is very extraordinary,' he had often thought to himself, 'that beautiful women have very little brain.'

When they first attracted him, it was most usually because of something witty they had said or more often they had made it very clear that they desired him.

If there was one thing he really disliked, it was the endless repetition of what had happened yesterday and the day before that.

He was always seeking something different and so far with women he found that there was nothing new or different in any of them.

They attracted him, he admitted, physically, but he found them, after a relatively short time, extremely dull in every other way.

What was more, most of them had some irritating habits, like twisting their rings or repeating what he had just said and it was as if they changed the whole sense by their own interpretation of it.

In the last few years he had found, when he was bored, it was easy to make an excuse to visit Paris, better still to travel to Scotland where he would be offered sport like fishing or shooting.

This invariably would take his mind off what he found monotonous and dreary.

Now it was summer and there was no question of sport and he therefore found what he enjoyed more than anything else was to swim in his own lake or to ride his own horses over his own broad acres.

He always made up his mind very quickly.

Having sent a messenger ahead on a fast horse, he left London as soon as he had finished breakfast and dealt with his voluminous correspondence.

He could trust his efficient secretary to cope with the ordinary mail like bills, advertisements and those who thanked him for his hospitality.

But there were also private letters, some of them scented, which only he could answer.

Today, however, he had been able to leave rather quicker than usual.

He was driving a new team of four that had been a recent purchase at Tattersalls and he thought it would be amusing to attempt to beat the record between his house in London and his house in the country.

It demanded all his concentration and it was only as he turned in through the great iron gates and started up the drive that he recalled the difficulties he had encountered on his last visit with his daughter Priscilla.

He had in fact been very angry and he had found that, because of her behaviour, two Governesses had left.

He remembered he had dismissed some in the past as being incompetent and had also listened to several who had been extremely rude about his daughter's demeanour.

He was tired of London and rather listless and he hoped that there would not be any dramas to cope with at The Court.

He almost prayed that he would not have to dismiss another Governess or be told by her in no uncertain terms why she was leaving.

When he drew up his team outside the front door, he was aware that he had broken his own record.

As the Head Groom came running from the stables followed by two other grooms, he remarked,

"I have brought you something really worth having, Abbey. This are the finest team I have ever had."

"They certainly be fine to look at, my Lord."

"I thought you would think so, that is why I could not resist them, although I don't mind telling you they cost me a pretty penny."

"But if you've broken the record, my Lord, then they be worth all you paid for 'em and a great deal more!"

The Marquis laughed.

"You are quite right, Abbey."

He went into the house to be greeted by the butler.

"It's very good to see your Lordship back," he said. "We were beginning to think you'd forgotten us."

"No, I have not, Harris, and it's wonderful to see so many flowers in the garden. I must certainly congratulate Greenhill on such a display."

"He was hoping your Lordship'd be pleased."

"Pleased, I really am delighted. Now where is her Ladyship?"

"At the lake, my Lord, with the new Governess."

Harris, who had been at The Court ever since the Marquis was a small boy, was about to say what a success Miss Lawson was, then he thought it would be wise to let the Marquis find it out for himself.

The difference in Lady Priscilla had, of course, not gone unnoticed by the rest of the staff.

At first they had been somewhat quizzical about the alterations Miss Lawson had made, but now they had to admit that her Ladyship was a different child.

All Harris said was,

"Her Ladyship was expecting your Lordship to be here about teatime. It'll be a nice surprise for her that your Lordship's appeared so early."

"I hope so," the Marquis said a little doubtfully.

He was remembering that the last time he had come home his daughter had refused to leave the nursery.

He had had to go up to her and there she had told him violently that she hated lessons and had no intention of doing them.

He had reproved her for having sent away another Governess, but she had merely said that she hated them all, as much as she hated her lessons.

The Marquis had been very angry and finally she had flounced into her bedroom and slammed the door. He had felt then that anything more he said would not only be unpleasant but useless and he had therefore left the house without saying goodbye to her.

On the long drive back to London he had wondered what he could do with his daughter in the future and it was obvious that no Governess could cope with her.

He had no difficulty in deciding not to ask any of his relatives to come to his assistance, as it was obvious to him that they would not be any more successful than he was in trying to tell the child what to do.

Also he disliked intensely having to admit he had failed in being the sort of father they expected him to be.

'I ought to love my daughter and she ought to love me,' he told himself.

But he knew that they had only to be together for there soon to be a ferocious quarrel in which they both inevitably lost their tempers.

'I can only hope,' he said to himself, as he walked down towards the lake, 'that things will be different from last time. If they are not, I will have to leave, beautiful though my home is at this time of year.'

*

Now, as the Marquis picked her up and she hugged him, he thought it could not be the same child who had flounced into her bedroom.

"So you have been swimming," he finally asked.

"And I can swim now, Daddy," Pepe said excitedly. "I can really swim, just like a fish!"

"A rather big fish," the Marquis smiled. "You must be careful you are not caught!"

Pepe laughed.

"There is no fisherman to catch me here and if there was I would dive under the water and he'd not see me!"

The Marquis thought that this was a very different conversation from any they had had in the past.

Then he looked down to the lake and saw that, as he expected, Pepe had not been alone.

The sun was glinting on Eleta's hair, turning it to gold.

She was not at the moment swimming, but she was still in the water watching Pepe greet her father.

For a moment the Marquis thought that he must be dreaming.

He had never seen anyone quite so lovely.

He could only think for one absurd moment that she was a mermaid who was there by mistake or maybe she was just an apparition that emanated from his imagination.

Then, as Eleta started to swim slowly towards the hut, he realised that she was indeed real and human, but he thought she was far too lovely to be anything but a visitor.

Pepe still had her arm round his neck.

"How did you get here so early, Daddy?"

"I came with some new horses I want you to see. They are perfectly matched and it's my fastest time ever."

"I have a new horse," Pepe bubbled, "he is called Silver Star and he is very very fast."

"A new horse?" the Marquis asked dramatically.

Then, as Eleta stepped out of the water and onto the grass, he looked at her with astonishment.

The soft blue bathing dress she wore revealed the perfection of her figure and he thought that he had never seen anyone quite so perfect or so beautiful.

"Who is that?" he asked Pepe in a low voice.

"She is my new Governess. She is very clever and I love her. We have a lot of surprises for you, Daddy."

The Marquis thought that the new Governess was certainly a surprise in herself and, as she slipped into the hut, he suggested,

"You had better finish dressing and then we will go back to the house and you must tell me everything you have learnt since I have been away."

Then, as if his memory jolted him, he asked,

"The last occasion I was here there was an elderly woman who was your Governess. I cannot remember her name, but she told me that she was leaving."

"Oh, she left and the one after her left and so did the one after that," Pepe answered. "They were all horrid, ugly, nasty people and they tried to teach me all the things I did not want to learn."

"And when did this one come to you?"

"She has not been here very long, but you will be very surprised at what I can do. She tells me beautiful, beautiful stories."

The Marquis put his daughter down on the ground.

"Now hurry up and dress," he urged. "I want to hear everything you have done. It all sounds exciting."

"It's all very exciting, Daddy, and I have a special surprise for you."

She was thinking as she ran towards the hut that it was a pity that her father had come back so soon.

It was, of course, Eleta who had said to her,

"When your father does return, you must be able to play the piano to him. He will be astonished that you can."

Pepe was thinking that if he had come next week or the week after she would be really good, but now she could play a little, which before she had not been able to do at all.

Inside the hut Eleta was nearly dressed.

"We thought your father would not be here until this afternoon," she said.

"I know and I have told him that we have lots of surprises for him and I kissed him as you told me to do."

"I saw you do that and you did it very well. Just remember that your father has no one to make a fuss of him now he is back in his home. All men want a woman to listen to them and to do things with them."

Pepe put her head on one side.

"What sort of things?"

"Like riding with him and asking his advice and, of course, looking pretty and smiling as you are now."

"I will be very very nice to Daddy, I promise."

"We must both be. Or he might send me away and say he wants an older and stricter Governess for you."

"Oh, he must not say that, he must not!" Pepe cried. "I love you and I don't want to lose you."

"Then you must make him think how happy he is to be with us. Make a very big fuss of him and make him feel important, which of course he is."

"I will try, I promise you I will try. I know you are frightened that he might send you away, Eleta, but, if he does, I will come with you."

"You must not say that to him. Just make him feel it is fun to be here in the country and that he has a very clever and very loving daughter."

Pepe gave a little laugh and, after Eleta had done up her dress at the back, she ran out of the hut.

Her father was standing where she had left him by the water and she slipped her hand into his and said,

"I am so glad you have come back, Daddy."

"You used to call me 'Papa'," he queried,

"Miss Lawson said 'Papa' sounded so very stiff and 'Daddy' was a more affectionate word."

"I think that Miss Lawson is quite right, although it never occurred to me before."

"She always thinks of something new and exciting and please, Daddy, be very kind to her because she is very frightened you might send her away."

Pepe's fingers tightened on his hand as she added,

"You won't do that, will you?"

"No, of course not," the Marquis replied. "If she is teaching you and you are happy, that is all that matters."

"Thank you, Daddy, thank you. I have learnt a lot with Miss Lawson and there is lots more to learn."

"Of course there is," he agreed.

Eleta came out of the hut and he thought again as she walked towards him that he had never seen anyone quite so lovely.

Then, as Eleta held out her hand, she said,

"As I expect Pepe will have told you, my Lord, I am the new Governess and I hope that you will approve of everything we have done."

"I am sure I will. My daughter seems to be happy and that is more important than anything else."

"I was hoping that was what you would think."

"I am very very happy," Pepe cried, pulling at her father's arm. "We have so many surprises for you."

The Marquis looked at Eleta.

"Is this some new method of learning I have not heard about?" he enquired.

"No, I think it is something that comes naturally in a different way to different people," Eleta replied.

It was not the answer he expected and he asked,

"Are you really suggesting that the lessons that are more or less laid down in the books are out of date?"

"Not exactly out of date, but I think, my Lord, you must realise that we are all made differently and none of us are the same. So what we are taught may be manna from Heaven for one person, while for another it is almost the fires of Hell."

The Marquis chuckled.

"I have not heard that before and you must explain it to me in more detail."

"I think you will be able to see the difference for yourself," Eleta suggested.

As they were walking into the house, the Marquis thought that she was not only too young to be a Governess but certainly too beautiful.

Now that her hair was arranged neatly at the back of her head, it made her look very youthful and he thought her features, as he glanced at her, were almost classical.

It then struck him that she could not be real and she might in fact have dropped down from Olympus.

As they walked on, Eleta said,

"I only wish it was true. When I first saw Mount Olympus, I was disappointed. Then I knew that the spirits of the Gods and Goddesses are still there, just as they are all over Greece."

The Marquis was astonished.

"You have read my thoughts!" he exclaimed,

"I too was surprised that I did," Eleta replied. "It does just happen sometimes. But let me say, not often."

They walked on for a little while and Pepe was still holding her father's hand and then Eleta said,

"I have been planning for some time to tell Pepe about Greece and its superb Gods and Goddesses that have altered the thinking of almost every country in the world."

"And you think that would be a valuable part of my daughter's education?"

"I think it is something we all yearn for and some of us are lucky enough to discover." Eleta answered.

The Marquis again thought he must be dreaming. This could not be happening to him in his own home.

Was it just his imagination?

Was she actually a Goddess from Mount Olympus walking beside him and teaching his daughter?

CHAPTER SIX

Eleta had, when she first arrived, been very careful not to refer too much to religion.

She had learnt in the Convent that quite a number of the girls were sick of being taken to Church every day and disliked being made to say prayers and being given long and boring lessons on Church history.

So she had only occasionally mentioned angels and had not enquired whether Pepe said her prayers at night.

Then they had talked about the angel called 'Pepe' who looked after her.

Eleta began to think that she should suggest they went to Church on Sunday or to pray in the charming little Chapel attached to the house.

She had discovered it when she was exploring some of the other rooms and she thought that it was one of the prettiest private Chapels she had ever seen.

It was a joy to see anything quite as beautiful as the Chapel and it had been built at the same time as the house.

The Adam brothers had indeed excelled themselves in making a Chapel that was really lovely, but also had an atmosphere of holiness which you felt from the moment you walked through the door.

When Eleta was talking to the Head Gardener about the hut at the lake, she had also asked him if he would send more flowers into the house.

"I would like as many as you can spare me," she had said, "for the room we use as a schoolroom. I would also like to see the Chapel decorated as I am sure you do it beautifully."

The flattery succeeded and the next day when she peeped into the Chapel she saw there were not only flowers on the altar but on all the windowsills.

It made the Chapel look even more glorious and she thought that she must take Pepe there more often.

It would be a mistake to do anything to antagonise Pepe, but Eleta wanted her to feel how useful prayer could be to her and how much it would mean in her future life.

It had certainly not helped her up to the present and Eleta was certain that the Governesses had very likely told her, as they had Mrs. Hill, that she was a child of the devil.

After they had walked back from the lake with the Marquis, she said that she was going to go upstairs to tidy herself for luncheon.

"I will come up in a moment," Pepe said. "I just want to show Daddy the picture that came back last week from being cleaned and which is in his study."

Eleta thought that this was certainly a new step in the relationship between father and daughter and without more ado she disappeared.

She ran down the corridor that led to the Chapel and when she went in she felt immediately the atmosphere of holiness that to her was very vivid.

She then knelt down and prayed fervently that the Marquis would accept her and she would not be sent away.

'Please God, please let me stay here,' she prayed. 'If I go back, I know I will never be able to find another position as nice as this. If Step-papa finds me, whatever I say, I will still have to marry the Duke.'

She felt as if her prayers went up to Heaven and, when she opened her eyes and looked at the Cross on the altar, she felt that she was being blessed.

Then, because she dared not linger, she ran all the way to her new bedroom on the first floor.

She looked in the mirror and saw that her hair, after being pinned up in such a hurry, was untidy and she then rearranged it making it a little more severe because she thought she would then look more like a proper Governess.

She had decided to wear, when she first met the Marquis, a dress that was very simple, but, because it had been such a lovely day, she had put on one of her summer frocks that was a pale blue scattered with pink flowers.

There was no time now to change, so she hurried downstairs, just in case luncheon had been announced.

She had timed it well because Pepe was still with her father in his study looking at the picture of horses that he had sent to be cleaned and reframed.

As Eleta was about to enter, Pepe was saying,

"I am going to ride a horse as big as that one day, Daddy, and then I will be able to race you."

"I expect you will win," the Marquis said, "simply because I will be getting so old I will have to ride slowly."

Pepe laughed.

"You will not be as old as all that."

"Judging by the rate you have jumped from a pony to a horse, Pepe, I expect you will be challenging me on the Racecourse in the next year or two."

"I hope so and Miss Lawson says I ride very well."

Then, as they had no idea that Eleta was standing just inside the door, the Marquis said,

"Tell me, is your new Governess a good rider? I was surprised to learn that she rides, as none of your other Governesses did."

"Oh, they were ghastly old women who would not have been able to ride a donkey." Pepe said scornfully. "Miss Lawson is very good. The grooms in the stables are astonished at how well she can handle your horses."

"She has been riding my horses!"

"Only because they needed more exercise than they were having," Eleta remarked from the doorway.

The Marquis turned round.

She thought perhaps that he would be irritated and she went forward saying,

"Please don't be angry with me for doing so. But there were too many for the older of your grooms and the young ones were too frightened to ride them."

For a moment she thought that the Marquis was annoyed and then unexpectedly he smiled.

"You are certainly a surprise in every possible way, Miss Lawson. I did not know that I had given orders to my secretary for a new groom as well as another Governess!"

"I am sorry if I have done anything wrong, my Lord, but, when your Head Groom saw me ride, he knew I was used to horses and I took out a different one each day."

Before the Marquis could speak, Pepe pushed her hand into his.

"You must not be angry with Miss Lawson," she said. "She has tried in every way to make things happy and better for me and I cannot lose her."

There was almost a pregnant silence and then the Marquis replied,

"No, of course not, I must thank her for being so considerate not only to my daughter but to my horses."

"Please," Eleta begged, "when you are not here, my Lord, may I go on riding them?"

The words came out before she could control them.

The Marquis looked at her.

She had no idea how lovely she looked with the sun coming through the windows turning her head to gold and her blue eyes were looking pleadingly up at him.

For a moment they just gazed at each other and then something passed between them that Eleta could not put into words.

Then in the silence Harris announced at the door,

"Luncheon is served, my Lord."

Pepe gave a little skip of joy.

"I am hungry," she cried, "and I am sure Monsieur Téyson has something delicious for us."

The Marquis looked surprised when she mentioned the chef by name, but he did not question it.

He and Pepe walked hand in hand towards the door, but Eleta hesitated and said,

"Maybe you would rather, my Lord, have luncheon alone with Pepe and I can, of course, have mine upstairs."

"No, of course not. I want you to have luncheon with me and tell me how you are educating my daughter and I must congratulate you that she can now swim."

"I can swim very well," Pepe boasted. "In fact I can go right across the lake to the other side and then back again almost as quickly as Miss Lawson can."

"It is certainly something new," the Marquis said, "to find that one of the Governesses is bathing. I always suspected that some of them were rather worried at having a bath!"

He was speaking jokingly, but Pepe piped up,

"They were horrid women and taught me nothing!"

Her father looked at her.

"I thought it was you who refused to learn."

"Only because they tried to teach me stupid boring things."

"But Miss Lawson is different?"

"She is very very different and she has taught me lots and lots I did not know before. Tomorrow when you have breakfast I am going to say, '*bonjour, mon père*'."

The Marquis looked at her in astonishment.

"Are you telling me that you are learning French?"

"I know lots of French words."

Listening to this conversation, Eleta could not help praying that Pepe would not forget them.

When they reached the dining room, the Marquis sat down at the head of the table.

Pepe sat on his right and Eleta on his left.

She realised that Monsieur Téyson had certainly done his best where the food was concerned.

They started off with a prettily decorated dish of smoked salmon and, when the second course arrived, Pepe exclaimed before anyone else could speak,

"Oh, it is *boeuf en croûte*! One of my favourite dishes and you will love it, Daddy."

The Marquis looked at Eleta and asked,

"Does she really know any French?"

"We started where I thought was the right place – at the dining table. Your chef has been most co-operative."

The Marquis continued to be surprised when Pepe greeted the pudding with a cry of '*isles flottantes*'.

When the coffee came in, she exclaimed that the *petits fours* were new and the chef must have made them especially for her father.

Pepe chatted away about where she had ridden on her new horse and told her father that one of the mares had a foal and that she and Miss Lawson were now thinking of a good name for it.

"I think I will have to help you there," the Marquis suggested, "as I have to look at its pedigree."

Pepe laughed.

"That is exactly what Miss Lawson said to me and I think if all the foals have pedigrees I should have one too."

"But you have one," the Marquis answered.

"Not with my name on it. Miss Lawson wanted to see the Family Tree – and it ends with you."

"That is most remiss of me and I must apologise. Your name will be put on it immediately and I will have a special copy made for the schoolroom."

"That will be lovely. Of course I want to be on our Family Tree. One day, Miss Lawson says, you will give me a brother and he, when you eventually die, will be the next Marquis."

Eleta thought that this was rather embarrassing, but to her relief the Marquis laughed.

"I must say," he said, "I never expected to find my very difficult and in the past naughty daughter rebuking me about our Family Tree!"

"We saw it hanging in the library," Eleta added, "and, as it is such a magnificent one, I thought Pepe would be proud to be on it. We started at the top and it was only when we reached the bottom we found it ended with you."

"As I have said, I will put right immediately. I am just wondering, Miss Lawson, how many other things you have found different from what they should be."

"Perhaps I had better break it to you before anyone else does, my Lord, but I thought, and I do hope you agree with me, that Pepe is too old to be shut up in the nursery at the top of the house. We therefore moved down to the first floor and we are actually occupying the King's suite."

For a second the Marquis just stared at her and then he exclaimed,

"The King's suite! You are certainly going to the top, Miss Lawson."

"What could be more appropriate for your lovely daughter, my Lord?" she replied.

For a moment she thought that he was going to be angry and then he laughed.

"You are now leaving me breathless, confused and, of course, amazed. Tell me what else you have done. Or should I try guessing?"

"I think," Eleta replied, "that Pepe has something very special to tell you that she is learning, but you have come back a little too soon. It would have been a better surprise if you had stayed away perhaps another fortnight."

"I am prepared to believe anything at the moment! Tell me, Pepe, what is this secret?"

"I think it would be best, Pepe, if you showed your father what you can do instead of trying to put it into words," Eleta suggested.

"Yes, yes, we will take him there as soon as he has finished his coffee. And I want to eat one more *petits four* before I leave."

"You can eat as many of them as you like, while Miss Lawson and I finish our coffee."

Pepe managed to devour two *petits fours* and then she jumped off her chair saying,

"Now Daddy, we are going to give you a surprise and I have been working very hard to make it for you."

Eleta realised that the Marquis had not the faintest idea what it could be.

But he was obviously amazed at the change in his daughter and he could not help looking at her as if he was not quite certain that she was real.

They left the dining room and then Pepe led him to the music room.

Fresh flowers and plants had been put in after the gardeners heard that the Marquis was arriving and they scented the air exquisitely.

She would have helped Pepe onto the stool in front of the piano, but she insisted,

"No, you must play first, as you always play to me. Then I will play the special tune that I have composed for Daddy."

Eleta could see that the Marquis was looking even more astonished than he had at luncheontime and then he sat down in the comfortable chair near the piano.

Without arguing, she ran her fingers over the keys and played one of the delightful romantic waltzes that had thrilled her when she went to the opera in Paris.

She saw that the Marquis was listening intently and when she finished he clapped and Pepe clapped too.

Eleta rose from the stool and turned to Pepe,

"Now it's your turn. Don't be in a hurry, it's a very beautiful tune you have composed and I want your father to hear every note of it."

Pepe sat on the stool. Her legs were not quite long enough to reach the pedals, so Eleta moved her carefully into position.

Then, as she knew that it meant so much to her, she prayed that Pepe would remember the notes which she had found out herself.

Her prayer was certainly answered.

Pepe played the piano with only one hand and she managed to make the tune, which she thought had come to her in her sleep, realistic to her father.

It was short, but it was recognisably a good tune.

When she finished, she looked at the Marquis and he clapped his hands and enthused,

"Wonderful, darling, and a lovely tune. One day when you have finished it, we will get it published so that everyone can play it and it will make them as happy as you have made me."

"You really like it, Daddy?" Pepe asked.

"Of course I like it. I had no idea that I had such a talented daughter who is also a musician."

"That is what I want to be and Miss Lawson says there is no doubt I will be."

The Marquis rose from his chair and, picking his daughter up from the stool, kissed her.

"I am very proud of you, Pepe. It is something I have never said before, but I have a feeling I will be saying it many times in the future."

"Do you really think it's a pretty tune?" she asked.

"It's lovely. I promise you when you have finished it, it will be printed and there will be a picture of you on the cover."

Pepe gave a cry of delight.

"Did you hear that, Miss Lawson?" she asked.

Then, looking at the Marquis, Eleta said,

"I am so glad you are pleased with it, my Lord."

"Pleased is not the right word. I am just astonished, delighted and very grateful to you."

He spoke with a deep note of sincerity in his voice.

As his eyes met Eleta's, he was aware that there were tears in her eyes.

He wondered how she could care so much for a child she had only known for a very short time.

At the same time she was so attractive, in fact so beautiful, it was difficult to imagine her as a Governess.

"Now I think," he said aloud, "we should ask Miss Lawson to play for us again. I promise you, Pepe, I will not neglect my music in the future as I have done in the past."

Pepe stepped down from the platform and, as Eleta sat down on the stool, the Marquis took Pepe on his lap in the armchair.

"Are you really pleased with my music, Daddy?" she asked him again. "I worked very hard at it because Miss Lawson knew it would be such a surprise for you."

"It has been a real surprise and the most marvellous present you could possibly have given me."

Pepe kissed his cheek.

"That is just what I wanted you to say to me."

The Marquis tightened his arm round her and Eleta began to play.

As she was feeling swept away by the music that came from this perfect piano, it seemed to carry her into a magical world where everyone was happy and no one was frightened.

She played again the music she had heard and loved in different countries, including Greece where naturally she connected it with Apollo.

It suddenly struck her as she was playing that the Marquis was undoubtedly the most handsome man she had ever met.

With his broad forehead, his clear features and, perhaps most important of all, his steady eyes, he looked different from any other man she had ever imagined.

'He looks exactly as a Marquis should look,' she told herself.

Then, because she was afraid of being a bore, she stopped playing and the Marquis, who had sat very quietly with Pepe in his arms, said,

"Thank you very much. I recognised some of the tunes you played and I thought you made them even more effective than the orchestras applauded all over Europe."

"Thank you, my Lord, I don't believe a word of it, but I am delighted at such a marvellous compliment."

"Actually what I said is true, but before the day comes to an end I would like to go into the garden and see the flowers."

"They are very very beautiful," Pepe sighed.

"Then you must show them to me, darling."

He walked towards the door, leading his daughter by the hand and then he looked back.

"I want you to come too, Miss Lawson. I have a feeling, but I may be wrong, that you know more about flowers than I do and I rather fancied myself up to now."

Eleta laughed.

"I think you are expecting too much," she replied.

"I am prepared for another shock," the Marquis said, "and, after what has happened already today, I would not be surprised if we do not find angels descending from Heaven and waiting for us on the lawn!"

"That would be exciting, Daddy," Pepe said. "And maybe my angel, who is called 'Pepe', will be with them."

"Your own angel? Have you one?"

"When Miss Lawson and I were frightened of the thunderstorm, she told me that both her angel and my angel were looking after us."

"If your angel is called 'Pepe'," the Marquis asked, "then what is Miss Lawson's called?"

Eleta drew in her breath, but to her relief she heard Pepe say,

"That is a secret. As I promised not to tell anyone, I cannot even tell you, Daddy."

"Of course you must keep your promise, darling."

"That is what Miss Lawson told me."

They walked into the garden.

The many flowers were even more stunning, Eleta thought, than when she arrived and the Marquis certainly knew a great deal more about them than she did.

She learnt that many of them had been brought by him from Nepal and from other places in the world where orchids are particularly fine and unusual.

As always, Pepe was fascinated by the fountain and she was standing staring up at it when the Marquis asked in a low voice to Eleta,

"How could you possibly have achieved this? How could you have transformed my naughty daughter into this charming and intelligent girl I can hardly recognise?"

"I am glad you are pleased," Eleta replied shyly.

"Of course I am pleased, but tell me how you have done it."

Eleta looked towards Pepe.

115

She was standing with her head thrown back to gaze up at the top of the rising water and it was a picture that any famous artist would have wanted to paint.

Then, almost as if the Marquis had compelled her to answer his question, she said,

"I believe that what Pepe wants is love."

There was silence for a moment and then he said,

"That is something we all want, but, if it is real, it is difficult to find."

They had tea in the conservatory, where many of the rarest and most unusual plants the Marquis had brought back from abroad were just coming into bloom.

Pepe was delighted with them and her father tried to teach her the names of some of them.

"You must not make it too hard for us, my Lord." Eleta protested. "We have so much going in and out of our brains at the moment that I am afraid, if you push us too hard, there will be a collision."

"I cannot believe that where you are concerned. If this is the new method of teaching the young, I can only say I will recommend it to every teacher in the world."

Eleta laughed as he continued,

"Then they will erect a statue of you outside every school!"

"What a thought!" she cried, "but as everyone is so different, you cannot make it dull and formal by writing it all down."

The Marquis nodded in agreement.

"I am quite convinced," Eleta went on, "after my experience here that the only real way of teaching is from mind to mind and, of course, from heart to heart."

"You are absolutely right, Miss Lawson, but I don't think anyone except you has ever thought of it that way before."

"I am certain they have, but they have not had the same material as I have had with Pepe, nor such enchanting surroundings in which to teach her."

She paused for a moment before she added,

"Everything is so beautiful here, that anyone who lives amongst it must inevitably become beautiful too."

"That is what I used to hope," the Marquis replied, "and what I now believe."

Eleta turned to look at him to see if he was telling the truth as he saw it.

When their eyes met there were somehow no words with which they could express what they were feeling.

It was after tea that Eleta proposed,

"I think as it is such a lovely evening we must have one more look at the sun sinking behind the trees and then we must go upstairs."

"And leave me?" the Marquis asked.

"I am afraid so, my Lord. I think it's a mistake, because we ride so early in the morning, that Pepe should be late in going to bed."

She looked at the clock and continued,

"Her supper will be ready for her at seven o'clock."

"Do you eat at the same time?" the Marquis asked.

"Yes, of course," Eleta replied.

"Well I think tonight, as I am alone," he answered, "you should have dinner with *me*."

Eleta looked at him in surprise.

"Are you sure that is wise, my Lord?" she asked. "It is very unusual, I know, for a Governess to have dinner in the dining room, although it is permissible for her to appear there for luncheon."

"There is no one here to be shocked or curious. I have some work to do first, but I should be delighted if you will be my guest at eight-thirty, Miss Lawson."

"Of course I want to accept," Eleta said, "but you must realise that it will surprise the staff."

The Marquis smiled.

"I should have thought that what you have achieved already is enough to keep them talking until Christmas," he said. "Therefore one more shock is neither here nor there."

"Then, my Lord, I am delighted to accept your kind invitation and I hope Pepe may come and say goodnight to you before she goes to her own room."

"I will be in the study waiting for her."

Pepe, although she protested that she had no wish to go to bed, was really very tired. It had been an exciting day and, as Eleta was aware, the heat had taken its toll.

The chef sent her up a particularly appetising dish of her favourite fish and that was followed by a deliciously light pudding and two or three even more unusual *petits fours* than she had had before.

"I will thank Monsieur tomorrow," Pepe said, "and tell him that he has beaten all records with the food he gave Daddy at luncheon and the special cakes at tea."

"I think you will have to go and tell him how clever he has been as soon as your father leaves," Eleta suggested.

"When is he going?" Pepe enquired.

"I have no idea, but I expect he will in a day or so."

"I love having him here and I think Papa is very nice now and not cross and disagreeable as he was before."

"You must forget all that," Eleta said. "You must remember he had all those tiresome women telling him how bad and naughty you were and, because they were supposed to be experienced, he believed them."

She smiled at Pepe before she went on,

"It was not his fault he did not find out how clever you really are and how many new and exciting things you will have to show him the next time he comes home."

Pepe was immediately interested.

"What will they be?" she asked.

"I am not quite certain yet, because you are such an unusual person in yourself."

She saw that Pepe did not understand exactly and she held up her hand.

"Firstly," she said touching her little finger, "you have proved yourself good enough to ride almost as well as your father and secondly you have learnt quite a lot of French in a very short time.

"Thirdly you are swimming exceedingly well and fourthly and, perhaps the most important of all, you have composed a tune which is all your own and which no one has ever heard before."

Pepe listened entranced.

"Am I really as clever as that?" she asked.

"You are much cleverer, but we have to find out what special gifts God has given you and how you can use them to delight or help other people."

"Is that what I ought to do?

"Of course it is, but some people are so selfish and don't give enough of themselves to others. And you, Pepe, have so much to give. But first we have to discover it."

"That will be exciting!" Pepe exclaimed.

"Now run down and kiss your father goodnight, but don't stay long because I have a special story to tell you when I tuck you up. Then I have to have a bath and change my dress before I have dinner with him."

"Then I will hurry because it would be a mistake to keep Daddy waiting."

Eleta smiled.

"It is clever of you to understand, but I knew you would. We both have to think of other people as well as ourselves.

"Yes, of course," Pepe said happily. "Now I will go down and give Daddy a big kiss."

"And tell him that you love him," Eleta added as the child reached the door.

"I do love him," Pepe called back, "but I also love you, Eleta, more than anyone else in the whole world."

She did not wait for Eleta's reply, but ran down the large staircase into the hall.

When Eleta had put Pepe to bed, she just had time to enjoy the bath that had been brought to her room.

Then she put on one of the prettiest evening gowns she bought in Paris.

She was so glad that she had included them in her luggage, even though she had thought at the time it was very unlikely she would have a chance of wearing them.

Now she took a last look at herself in the mirror and she certainly did not look like any Governess or teacher she had ever seen!

She wondered if perhaps the Marquis would think she was pretending to be more important than she actually was and then she told herself, if he did think that, it was entirely his fault.

He should not have asked her, as a Governess, to have dinner with him, but he had the excuse that he wanted to discuss his daughter's future with her.

It was five and twenty minutes past eight when she walked into the blue drawing room where a footman had told her that the Marquis was waiting.

When Eleta came into the room wearing a dress of soft pink chiffon with a bustle of silver lace, the Marquis felt that she might have stepped out of a dream.

He watched her walk towards him and, when she reached him, he put a glass of champagne into her hand.

"Tonight we have to celebrate something extremely special," the Marquis began.

"What is that, my Lord?" Eleta asked.

"The change that you have made in my daughter. If I had not seen it with my own eyes, I would not have believed it was true but part of someone's imagination."

Eleta smiled.

"I am so glad you are pleased, my Lord."

"As I have told you before there are no words to express what I feel. I only know that today I have found my daughter and she is absolutely and completely different from the child I have known."

He picked up his own glass and held it up.

"I can only toast you for looking and being, as you quite obviously are, an angel from Heaven or a Goddess from Mount Olympus."

"I am delighted to be either and thank you very much. It's the finest compliment I have ever had."

"I am sure that you have had a great number of them," the Marquis replied in a different tone of voice.

"Not really," she replied. "I hope, my Lord, after all the encouraging things you have said about Pepe, that you will tell me what you are contemplating for her next."

"You can hardly expect me to think of anything better than you have done already. How is it possible that, looking so young, you could know exactly what to do with a child who everyone else told me was un-teachable?"

"Few children are really that unless they are driven to it by people who don't understand them. Because Pepe is very intelligent, she needs encouragement and guidance not condemnation, which as far as I can make out is all she received from the women who came here."

"And you succeeded magnificently where they had failed. Now I want you to tell me about yourself and why, looking as you do, you have become a Governess."

Before Eleta could think of an answer, to her relief dinner was announced.

They went into the dining room and, as might have been expected, the chef had made every possible effort. He produced a meal that the Marquis would not have found surpassed in any restaurant in Paris.

It was impossible to talk privately while they were at dinner with all the servants waiting on them and so they exchanged anecdotes about the different countries they had both visited.

The Marquis found it extraordinary that Eleta knew most of the countries in Europe and had also been to Africa and Egypt.

He did not say so, but he assumed that her parents must have been rich to be able to afford the expense of so much travelling.

And he supposed that for some reason they must now be bankrupt, which was why she was forced to take a position as a Governess.

When the servants left them to enjoy their coffee and liqueurs, the Marquis suggested again,

"Now that we are alone I want you to tell me about yourself. I cannot believe there is not some special reason for your taking a position as Governess."

"Why should you think that?" Eleta asked him.

"Because you have just told me how far you have travelled and the gown you are wearing must have cost a whole year's salary in your present position."

"Of course I should not have brought to your notice two things that are so expensive. I forgot that you would be astute enough to find it strange."

"Now tell me how you can do it."

Eleta shook her head.

"You must leave me my secrets, my Lord. All I can tell you is that I have never been so happy as I am at the moment here with Pepe. I am only afraid that you may send me away because in many ways I do admit to having turned the whole place upside down."

"And it is something I want you to continue doing," the Marquis said. "I could no more send you away now than blow down the house itself. What you have done for my daughter is beyond any words I can express in English or in any other language."

"What I have done is to bring out what is hidden in her, while the Governesses who came here before were too stupid to see it."

She paused for breath before she added,

"She is an unusual, exceedingly bright young lady with a vivid imagination. That I believe must be developed until she becomes her own original person, whom everyone who meets her will admire and love."

"And, of course, love is the most important thing of all. I know that you are thinking I did not love my daughter enough and left her with people who did not even try to understand her. There is no one to blame but me."

"You now understand, my Lord, and that is what that really matters. I was so terrified that you would not

123

accept me and insist on going back to everything that is conventional and expected of a child of that age."

"I understand you have brought out her character, her personality and with that her achievement."

He paused before he continued,

"Now you have said that she wants love and that, of course, we can be quite certain she will have from me and from you."

Because Eleta thought that perhaps he was getting a little personal, she added,

"The chef, because she attempts to speak to him in French, is determined she will enjoy her food. I can assure you what we have been eating lately would shock the smart world of Mayfair and doubtless arouse the disapproval of Her Majesty the Queen!"

The Marquis laughed.

"I find the food at Windsor Castle very ordinary and unimaginative."

"I doubt if they employ a French chef, my Lord."

"I think it was my mother who engaged him and she, as you can see from the house, enjoyed everything that was delicious and beautiful."

"It is what we all want and what we hope and pray that we are going to have," she said.

"It is certainly what you should have," he replied.

And once again they were looking into each other's eyes and it was very hard to look away.

CHAPTER SEVEN

The next morning they rose early as the Marquis had said that it was going to be very hot.

He therefore suggested they had breakfast at seven-thirty and went for a ride soon afterwards.

Eleta thought it was an excellent idea and then they could swim later in the cool water of the lake.

She was almost dressed when Pepe came bouncing into her bedroom.

"It will be exciting to go out with Daddy," she said.

"Of course it will, Pepe, and you will have to show him how well you ride Silver Star."

"I love Silver Star, but I think I will soon want a much bigger horse."

Eleta thought that this was doubtful, but she did not want to argue about it, so she just urged,

"Concentrate on showing your father how well you ride and don't forget to tell Silver Star before you start how lovely he is."

"I will tell him, of course I will tell him."

She ran down and found the Marquis in the hall.

"Good morning, darling Daddy," she cried. "It's so very exciting to be going riding with you."

"And I am looking forward to riding with you," the Marquis replied. "But come in and have breakfast first."

After breakfast he said to Pepe,

"Run ahead and see that the horses are ready for us. We will join you in a few minutes."

When Pepe had run off, he turned to Eleta,

"I want to ask you something. I am sending a man to London today with some letters and I thought I would like to buy Pepe a special present."

"That is a lovely idea," Eleta enthused.

"I was wondering what I should get her. Do you think a doll, would be right, Miss Lawson?"

"Actually I think what she would love more than anything else is a dog of her own."

"A dog of her own! I did not think of that."

"She should have something which she has to bath and brush and see that he has the correct food."

"In other words – another lesson."

"Of course it is," Eleta replied. "Pepe has to learn to think about other people. As she has no children of her own age to think about, a dog is the next best thing."

"Of course it is and you are very wise."

"There is a man in Chelsea," Eleta went on, "who has young dogs already house-trained and has, I am told, a large selection."

"Do you know the address?" the Marquis asked.

"Yes, I do, and I will write it down for you."

Eleta ran to the nearest room to the writing desk and wrote down the address, which she had remembered, and took it back to the Marquis.

As she handed it to him, he said,

"I was just thinking that you always give me an answer I don't expect. That is unusual in women and I find it very interesting."

Eleta was just going to reply when the Head Groom came running through the front door.

"My Lord! My Lord!" he cried. "Her Ladyship's been kidnapped!"

"*Kidnapped!*" the Marquis exclaimed.

"Yes, my Lord, and this be what they left behind."

He handed the Marquis a piece of dirty paper.

Without asking permission, Eleta bent over his arm to look at it and on it was written,

"*If you wants your dorter back, leave ten thousand p by pool in wood. If you come looking for her, she die.*"

The Marquis stared at the piece of paper as if he could not believe what was written on it.

Eleta gave a cry.

"Who are these men – and how have they – taken her?" she asked the Head Groom hesitatingly.

"Lady Priscilla were a-talkin' to 'er horse, Silver Star. I were inside the stable gettin' the 'orses ready for 'is Lordship and then these two men seized the reins and pulls her out into the paddock. And when I 'ears the stable boy shoutin' I goes out and 'e shows I the piece of paper. Then I sees them and her Ladyship disappearin' in the distance."

"I cannot believe it," the Marquis cried. "We must go after them at once!"

"You see what the note says," Eleta said, "and I think that would be a mistake. They might hurt Pepe."

"Then what are we to do?" the Marquis asked.

"I think, although they have not said so, that they are hiding in the cave," Eleta replied.

"The cave?" the Marquis questioned.

"Yes, the cave that I was told is dangerous. Pepe wanted to explore it, but I would not let her do so until I had talked to you about it first, my Lord."

"How can we be sure they will be there?"

"There is nowhere else for them to hide as far as I can see," Eleta replied, "and they would have from there a very good view of the wood where they want you to leave the money."

"Yes, that makes sense," the Marquis murmured.

He was staring at the paper as he was speaking as if he could hardly believe what he had read.

"I have another idea," Eleta said after a while.

"What can it be?" the Marquis asked.

"I will go to the cave alone to be with Pepe."

The Marquis stared at her.

"You would really do that, but they will take you prisoner as well."

"Now listen. It is coming to me as if someone is telling me what to do."

She thought, although she did not say so, that it was either God or Pepe's angel who was telling her that this was the only way to save Pepe.

The Marquis and the Head Groom were waiting in astonishment as she went on,

"What I will do when we think they are settled in the cave, which will not take them long, is to ride through the wood and over to the cave. They will see me coming and, when I reach them, I will say I have been sent by you as you have gone to collect the money from the bank."

"Supposing they are not there?" the Marquis asked sharply.

"I am almost sure that is where they will be," Eleta replied. "Strangely enough, when we rode past yesterday, I thought that I saw someone moving in the entrance and then felt that it was just the sunlight and my imagination."

"What am I to do?" the Marquis asked.

"What I think would be reasonable and, of course, we must take care they don't hurt Pepe, is to gather all the men you can trust and who own guns and then go round to approach the cave from behind."

"You mean so that they will not see us."

"Exactly," Eleta agreed. "It will take you quite a time, but if you go round by the road and then approach the cave from behind, I am sure you will not be seen, because behind it there are trees and I thought, although I only had a glimpse of them, that there are bushes too."

"Aye, they be there," the Head Groom said. "They makes it impossible for people to approach the cave that way unless they crawl through 'em."

"That is exactly what we want," Eleta exclaimed.

She looked up at the Marquis.

"If you and the men you can trust crawl up from the back, then I think if they are watching the wood for you to bring the money, they will have no idea that you are there until you suddenly come round to the front."

"I understand what you are saying. I suppose there is no other way of rescuing Pepe. How many men do you think there are, Abbey?"

The Head Groom shook his head.

"There be only two as took 'er Ladyship away," he replied, "but I'll ask the others who were groomin' the 'orses if they knows anythin' about 'em."

"This means they have read all the reports written on you in the newspapers," Eleta remarked. "They might have come from London to extort money from you."

"Perhaps it would be easier to give it to them – "

Eleta thought for a moment and then she replied,

"I still think I ought to be with Pepe. She will be terrified and you must decide the best way to rescue her. But the longer she is with them alone, the worse it will be."

"Yes, of course," the Marquis agreed. "At the same time I want to speak to the groom who was holding Silver Star when the men appeared."

"There is something I want to fetch from upstairs," Eleta said. "I will meet you in the stables."

The Marquis walked off with the Head Groom and she ran up the stairs to her bedroom.

She then opened the case where she had hidden her father's revolver. It had been locked after her dresses had been taken out and the revolver was lying on the bottom with its bullets beside it.

She loaded it and then thrust it into the front of her blouse.

As it was so hot, she had been intending to ride without a coat and she thought it would be a mistake to take a coat now as it would invite the men to search her.

They would not notice the revolver underneath her muslin blouse and actually it was very uncomfortable, but she did not worry about that.

She then had a sudden thought and went into the boudoir where all Pepe's toys had been taken.

Along with the doll's house and a number of dolls and some tin soldiers was a flag. It was only a small one and had obviously been used in one of her games.

The flag was a Union Jack and Eleta pulled it off the stick and tied on a large white handkerchief in its place.

Then she ran downstairs and out through the back door, as it was the quickest way to the stables.

The Marquis was already there talking to the stable boy, who had been holding Silver Star and the other boys were all listening intently to what he was saying.

As Eleta joined them, she heard him say,

"Them weren't black, but then them weren't white. Them looked foreign-like, if you knows what I mean."

The Marquis looked round at the others.

"Have any of you here seen any foreigners of that description in the village?"

Then an older stable boy piped up,

"Them be laughing in the shop as them says three men comes in and asks where Teringford Court be. Them be just opposite the gates and they thinks they be stupid."

"Did he say what they looked like?" the Marquis asked.

The boy scratched his head trying to remember.

"I thinks someone says them be foreign 'cos them talked in a funny way, but I weren't listening no more."

"I was sure when I read that note," Eleta said in a low voice, "that they are foreigners and now I think about it perhaps they are French Africans."

The Marquis stared at her.

"Why on earth should you think that?" he asked.

"They have written ten thousand pounds with a 'p' after it instead of the way we write it. That is exactly the way the Arabs in that part of Africa write."

"Perhaps you are right, but what is more important than anything else is that as far as we know now there are only three of them. Therefore we should have no difficulty in coping with that lot."

"I will be there to comfort and protect Pepe," Eleta insisted.

She looked at the Head Groom.

"Give me a horse," she asked him, "that will not be upset if it is tied up to a tree or post below the cave."

"There won't be much there, miss, but if you rides old Samson, he'll not wander away far and we'll 'ave no difficulty when we gets there in catchin' 'im."

"Then find me Samson quickly," Eleta urged.

She thought as she spoke that she was being rather presumptuous in giving orders with the Marquis present.

But he did not say anything and she said to him,

"Whatever you do, my Lord, you must not be seen approaching. If you are seen, they might try to take Pepe somewhere different. Or perhaps just dispose of her."

"You are quite certain," the Marquis said quietly so that only she could hear, "that you are doing the right thing in going to Pepe? It is very brave of you and I suppose I should really go myself."

"That would be disastrous. They would, I am sure, shoot at you even if they thought that you were bringing the money. As you can see, I am carrying a white flag and I think even Africans will understand what that means."

Abbey brought Samson out of the stable and the Marquis, without waiting for her to go to the mounting block, lifted Eleta onto it.

Then he whispered so that only she could hear,

"I think that you are the bravest and quite the most wonderful woman I have met in my whole life. I promise you we will not be very far behind and I would willingly pay twenty thousand pounds to save you and Pepe from having to go through all this."

"It is a challenge and we cannot allow them to get away with it," Eleta asserted.

She did not wait for him to answer, but rode away holding the white flag and because she had not put on a hat the Marquis thought that she looked extremely lovely with the sunshine again turning her hair to gold.

She looked very small on a very large horse and at the same time she was going into battle against the enemy.

He knew that he had to save her as well as Pepe.

He therefore started giving his orders sharply in a manner that made everyone start running to do what he asked of them.

Eleta did not hurry across the fields.

She thought if anyone was watching her they might be agitated into thinking she had an army behind her.

She passed through the wood thinking as she did so that the kidnappers had chosen exactly the right place to receive the money they expected.

The pool was protected by the trees and it would be difficult for anyone to hide there without being seen.

Then she was in the open fields where at the far end was the large stony hill and in the distance she could see the mouth of the cave.

Holding up her flag so that it was high above her head, she rode directly across the middle of the field.

She wondered if anyone was watching her and she began to pray that Pepe was not hurt and that she would reach her safely.

It was an eerie feeling to be aware that eyes were watching her from a darkness she could not see into.

At last she reached the foot of the hill and it was then that she realised that the whole of the lower part of it was of rock and only in the entrance at the top was there anywhere for a man to hide.

Eleta dismounted and knotted the reins so that they would not be in the way of Samson eating the grass.

Then she patted him and he made no effort to trot away. He merely looked for some good grass.

Then she began to climb up the rocks.

It was a slow process and by this time the sun was very hot and she felt breathless when she reached the top.

Then two men appeared out of the darkness of the entrance to the cave.

"What you want?" one of them asked harshly.

One look at them told her that she had been right in thinking they were Arabs.

As he was speaking in an almost unintelligible way in English, she answered him in French.

"I have come to tell you," she said slowly so that they could understand every word, "that his Lordship, the Marquis, has gone to the bank to fetch the money you have asked for his daughter. I have come to stay with her until he puts it down in the wood by the pool as you demanded."

"You be sure that he's goin' there and not a-comin' here?" the man asked.

To her relief he spoke in broken French, but she was sure that it was better than his English.

Fortunately, because she had been interested during the time she was in Africa, she had learnt a little of their language.

Now she repeated what she had said in French in what she was able to remember of Arabic.

The man laughed.

"You speak our language!"

"I think your country is very beautiful," she replied, "and I hope to go back there."

"That's what we hopes too," the man said. "And, when we goes back, we'll go back rich."

"You will be rich as soon as the Marquis can bring the money for you," Eleta told him in English. "But he does not have all the money in the house."

She was not certain if he understood this and so she therefore said it again both in French and Arabic.

Then, as they seemed to be pleased at what she had told them, she asked,

"Now may I please go to the child? She must be very frightened and I don't want her to be upset."

The two men looked at each other and then the first man shrugged his shoulders.

"I suppose it'll do no harm."

"Thank you, thank you," Eleta said. "I just want to tell her stories and keep her happy until her father gives you the money you have asked for."

"He'd better do that," the other man answered, "or he no see daughter again!"

Eleta took a few paces forward and he led the way.

The outer cave was low and very dark. It was like a tunnel and Eleta was thinking just how much it must have scared Pepe.

Then there was a light ahead and Eleta now found herself in a very large cave and there was sunlight seeping through some holes in the broken rocks of the roof.

She could understand why people had said it was dangerous, as, if they walked on top of the rocky roof, it would be easy to fall through, even if not down into the cave and they might easily break an arm or leg in an effort to save themselves.

Patches of light made it easy for her to see Pepe.

She was sitting on the floor at the far end of the cave with her feet tied together.

She gave a cry when she saw Eleta.

"It's you! It's you"

"Yes, it is me," Eleta said, running towards her and, kneeling down beside Pepe, she put her arms round her.

135

As she did so, Pepe burst into tears and she held her very close.

"It's all right," she whispered, "it's quite all right. I am here and I am going to stay with you until your father rescues us."

"I am frightened, so very frightened," Pepe wept.

"Of course you are, but I am sure you have been very brave and now we just have to wait here until your Daddy gives these men the money they have asked for. I can tell you, darling, that you are very very expensive!"

"They said they were asking for money for me and I was afraid Daddy would not give it to them."

"Of course he will," Eleta assured her.

The man who had led the way was still listening.

"Now the first thing I am going to do," Eleta said, "is to undo this rope which is round your legs."

"It's very tight," Pepe sobbed, "and it hurts me."

"I am sure it does."

Eleta waved to the man watching and asked,

"Please take this rope off the child's legs. She will not run away now I am here."

He seemed about to refuse and then Eleta said,

"Please, there cannot be any reason for her to be tied up now I am with her."

Somewhat grudgingly, she thought, he drew a knife from his pocket and with some difficulty he cut through the rope and Eleta took it away from Pepe's legs.

She was wearing her riding boots and the rope had been so tightly tied that despite the boots it must have been painful.

"Now we are comfortable," Eleta said, "and, as there is nothing but rocks around this place, we just have to make the best of it."

"How did you know – I was here?" Pepe asked.

"I guessed it because it seemed the only place they could really hide you and not be seen. Now what we have to do while we are waiting for your father is to hold hands and not be too afraid."

As she was talking, she realised that another man she had not seen before, joined the man watching them.

He spoke to him in Arabic which she understood and then he said to her in broken English,

"See no one comin'. Her said he gettin' money, put by pool."

"Take him long time to get big sum," the man who had been the guide muttered.

"More the better. Then we leave quick, ship sails tomorrow night."

Listening, this told Eleta that she had been right in thinking that they were Arabs. From the way they looked, she was sure that they came from the Western region of North Africa where she had stayed with her friends.

Pepe had now stopped crying and she wiped her eyes with her handkerchief.

"Why were you carrying my flag?" Pepe asked her. "And why have you made it white?"

"I will tell you a story about flags," Eleta said, "and I think it's something you will find interesting."

She started to tell her how flags were first used and how important they became in war. It took some time and Eleta realised, as she was making Pepe laugh, that now the two men at the entrance to the cave were listening to what she was saying.

They had even sat down on the ground, sitting in their traditional way on their heels.

Pepe, because Eleta had her arms round her, was leaning her head comfortably on her shoulder.

She was listening and apparently quite happy.

Then suddenly, at what seemed a long time later, when her voice was becoming quite hoarse from talking so long, the man she had first seen when she arrived came running down the cave.

"A man's come round corner," he called out, "and I thinks he be Marquis."

"He go to wood?" one of them asked.

"He be alone, but if he's up to tricks or take back money after we left, give him shot in leg so we get away."

He did not wait for the others to answer, but just as they understood, so did Eleta.

Without disturbing Pepe, she managed to take out her revolver.

Gently she put it where she could reach it quickly and then she started another story about a flag.

At the same time she was watching the men at the far end of the cave.

Each man, Eleta saw, produced a pistol.

Then they stood up and were watching the entrance.

She ceased speaking and there was silence.

Then she heard the voice of the third man and what she was sure was the Marquis asking him where Pepe was.

It was then, without waiting any longer, she fired at the two men.

There were two resounding reports that echoed and re-echoed in the cave.

Eleta shot the first man in the shoulder.

He screamed out and fell backwards, his gun falling from his hands.

Then she shot the other man in the right arm and he too dropped the gun he was holding.

At first he held his arm and then collapsed onto the ground.

It was then that another shot rang out.

Pepe screamed and hid her face against Eleta.

The Marquis then walked into the cave and he was holding a revolver in his hand. He saw Pepe and Eleta and hurried across the cave towards them.

He went down on one knee and asked Eleta,

"Who shot those other two men?"

She looked up at him and raised her hand and he saw the revolver she was holding.

Then Pepe cried,

"Daddy! Daddy! I am terrified. Take me away."

"That is exactly what I am going to do, my darling Pepe."

The Marquis lifted Pepe into his arms, kissed her and she hid her face against his shoulder.

"This is a horrible place," she whispered, "and I want to go home."

"That is just where I am taking you," the Marquis said, as he stood up and put his revolver into his pocket.

Then he held out his free hand to Eleta and she took it, feeling that the clasp of his fingers was very comforting.

As she climbed to her feet, the Marquis said,

"You are absolutely wonderful."

Then, as she looked up at him, as if it was the most natural thing in the world, he bent his head and kissed her on the lips.

For a moment they were absolutely still and Eleta felt that same sensation she had when she first saw him.

But now she knew it was love and she loved him.

The Marquis had turned away and was walking to where the men were moaning on the ground.

Even as he reached them, the Head Groom and two footmen came hurrying towards them.

"Are you all right, my Lord?" they asked.

"There are two casualties here, Abbey. Take them with the man I shot to the nearest Police Station and say that I will be there tomorrow morning to charge them."

"Very good, my Lord," the Head Groom replied.

Still carrying Pepe, the Marquis went ahead and once they were outside Eleta saw that there were four more men from The Court, all carrying guns and looking pleased with themselves.

The man the Marquis had shot was groaning and Eleta saw that he had been shot in the leg.

When the men from The Court saw Pepe in the Marquis's arms and Eleta beside him, they cheered.

He very carefully carried Pepe down the rocks and, as they reached the bottom, two more of his men brought the horses round from behind the entrance.

Eleta realised that the Marquis had taken her advice and he had approached the cave from the road, making a major detour, which was why he had taken so long.

She supposed they had really come as quickly as possible, but it seemed to her that she had been telling the stories about the flags for at least a hundred years!

"I think that Pepe should ride home with me," the Marquis said as they brought him his horse.

"I would like that, Daddy," Pepe murmured.

She had not spoken all the time that her father was carrying her down the hill and now she was safe, she raised her head from his shoulder.

140

"There is no hurry," the Marquis said. "At the same time, I don't know about you, but I am very hungry."

"It seems such a long time since breakfast," Eleta replied. "But we will be home for luncheon and I am sure that the chef will have thought of a delicious new dish."

"I was too frightened to be hungry," Pepe shivered.

"Of course you were, but we will make up for it by eating a really enormous luncheon. Then we will think of something rather quieter to do in the afternoon."

"It was very clever of Miss Lawson to shoot those two horrid men," Pepe piped up.

"Very clever indeed," the Marquis answered. "At the same time, I don't want to have to rescue you like this every day!"

"I was very frightened until she came and told me lovely stories about flags."

Eleta was standing beside them and she knew that the Marquis wanted to be quite certain the wounded men were being brought down from the cave.

Then the Head Groom came running in to say,

"I thinks they're past ridin', my Lord, and we'll have to fetch a cart for 'em."

"There is a farmer a little way down the road. If you tell him it's for me, there will be no problem about it. I am leaving you in charge while I take her Ladyship and Miss Lawson home."

"We'll do as your Lordship's orders and I knows where the nearest Police Station is."

"Report to me as soon as you get back, Abbey, and tell them I will be there early tomorrow. In the meantime they had better send for a doctor."

"I'll see to it, my Lord," he answered.

While they were talking, Eleta mounted her horse and they now set off.

The Marquis was going slowly as he had Pepe in front of him and had one arm round her.

They then rode through the wood and past the pool where the Marquis was to have placed the money.

As they did so, he said,

"I must thank you, Miss Lawson, for saving Pepe and indeed a large sum of money."

Eleta smiled.

"I was quite certain you would not have subjected yourself into parting with that sum without fighting for it!"

She recalled that he had said he would give twenty thousand pounds to save not only Pepe but herself.

Then she was vividly conscious once again of the feelings that had arisen within her when he kissed her.

It was only, she thought, because he was grateful to her for looking after Pepe, but she knew it was what she had felt about him from the first moment they had met.

'I love him,' she thought, 'but he will never love me and I must be careful not to let him know my feelings.'

They rode on and when they arrived at The Court it seemed that the whole staff was waiting in the hall.

"We've been really worried about your Lordship," Harris said, "and it's a great sight to see her Ladyship."

"We have won a most difficult battle, Harris," the Marquis said, "and now I want a glass of champagne and a very large luncheon."

Harris laughed.

"That'll be waiting for your Lordship in the dining room in five minutes."

"Pepe and I will just have time to wash our hands and make ourselves respectable," Eleta said.

She did not wait for the Marquis to answer, but she and Pepe ran towards the staircase.

"I am glad I am home," Pepe said, as they went into their room. "I was so scared until you came to save me."

"I hope you prayed to your angel to look after you."

"I did, but I knew, although it might be very very difficult, that you and Daddy would save me."

"Just forget all about it," Eleta suggested. "Wash your face and hands and we will hurry down to luncheon."

Five minutes later the Marquis handed Eleta a glass of champagne as they entered the drawing room.

"If anyone deserves it," he smiled, "you do."

"I want champagne too," Pepe asked.

"You can have a sip," the Marquis replied, "but I don't think you will like it as much as your lemonade."

He gave the child his glass, Pepe took a very small sip rather warily and then she wrinkled her nose.

"You are quite right, Daddy," she admitted, "I like my special lemonade that Monsieur Téyson makes with honey. It's much, much nicer than that."

"I will have to try it myself," the Marquis muttered.

He was talking to Pepe, but his eyes were on Eleta and, because she felt such intense feelings moving within her, she blushed as she looked away.

Luncheon was awaiting them and, although it was delicious, it was hard for her to think of anything but the man sitting beside her.

She was aware that he kept looking at her, although he was talking to Pepe.

They were just finishing their coffee and Pepe was devouring a *petit four* when Harris came into the room and said to the Marquis,

"There's a gentleman to see you, my Lord, on what he says is important business."

"I have no wish to see anyone today. Who is he?"

"He says his name, my Lord, is Mr. Warner."

Eleta was stunned into silence.

"Put him into the study and tell him to wait," the Marquis ordered. "I have no idea who he is."

Harris left the room.

Then Eleta said in a voice that did not sound like her own,

"It is my stepfather. Please, please will you hide me somewhere? I cannot imagine how he has traced me here."

The Marquis stared at her, but Pepe gave a little shriek,

"Your stepfather! The wicked man you have run away from. Oh, Daddy, we must hide her. He must not find her, he is a cruel horrid man."

"I don't understand. What is all this about?"

"I ran away from home and I told Pepe that is why I am here pretending to be a Governess. My stepfather wants me to marry a man who is fifty years old at least and whom I have never even met."

"She cannot marry him! She cannot!" Pepe cried, jumping up to run to her father's chair. "She will go away from us and we want her here."

The Marquis put his arm round Pepe's shoulders.

"Now tell me about this quietly," he suggested, "so that I understand what is happening."

"I am not a Governess and I have never been one," Eleta began.

He smiled, but did not interrupt and she went on,

"My mother and father are dead and my stepfather said that I am to marry a man I have never met, but who he thinks is very influential. I therefore went to an Agency in London and they offered me this job. That is why I am here. I have been so happy and I love Pepe."

"And I love Eleta," Pepe asserted. "So, Daddy, send this horrid man away and say she is to stay with us."

"Of course she must stay," the Marquis agreed.

"It is impossible if he knows I am here," Eleta said.

"Why?" the Marquis asked.

Eleta hesitated and then she told the truth.

"I am only twenty and he is my legal Guardian until I am twenty-one and that is not for another eight months."

"All I can say," the Marquis said quietly, "is that you are the most extraordinary, outstanding and brilliant twenty-year-old who has ever existed."

He paused before he added,

"And naturally I cannot lose you."

"Can you save her, Daddy?" Pepe almost screamed. "Because I want her, I want her here!"

"We both want her. So the sooner I get rid of him the better."

"But the law is on his side," Eleta mumbled.

"I am just thinking how I can defeat the law – "

"I think it's impossible unless I hide in the cellars and you say that the woman he is seeking has gone."

"I don't think that would be very effective, so I have a better plan."

"What is it?" Eleta asked.

"I think both you and Pepe will want to hear what I say to him. Let's go into the drawing room and you can hide behind the screen at the far end."

Before Eleta could reply, he gazed at Pepe and said,

"Now listen! If you make one sound, he will know you are there and that will spoil my plan for keeping Miss Lawson with us."

"I will be very very quiet," Pepe promised.

"Then come along. I know exactly what I am going to say and you can both hear it."

They went out of the dining room and saw Harris waiting outside.

"Wait for a moment," the Marquis said to him. "I am going into the drawing room and, when we are inside, you can bring Mr. Warner to me there."

"Very good, my Lord," Harris replied.

As they then entered the drawing room, Eleta saw, which she had almost forgotten, that at the far end was a large screen, finely carved and inlaid with mother-of-pearl.

Eleta and Pepe hurried across the room and they sat down on the floor behind the screen.

Eleta knew it would be impossible for anyone at the other end of the room to see them.

She put her finger to her lips, remembering as she did so how she had done that the first time she saw Pepe.

From that moment Pepe had become in many ways a changed child and now she snuggled up against Eleta, who put her other arm round her.

She felt as if they were both holding their breath.

The Marquis was standing at the other end of the room.

'I love him, I love him,' Eleta said to herself. 'Oh, please God, let me stay here. At least I will be near him and see him even if he will never love me.'

Then she felt again as if his lips were on hers and an amazing feeling was sweeping through her whole body.

'This is love,' she told herself. 'It is what I thought I would never find.'

She heard the door open and Harris announce,

"Mr. Cyril Warner, my Lord."

The Marquis held out his hand.

"I don't think we have met before, Mr. Warner, and I am wondering why you wish to see me so urgently."

"It has just come to my knowledge," he replied in a hard voice, "that my stepdaughter is here pretending to be a Governess, for which she is not trained and, I understand, has given a false name and lied about her age."

"Those are rather derogatory accusations and, as I find Miss Lawson extremely capable as a Governess to my daughter, I have no wish to lose her."

"Miss Lawson, as you call her," Cyril Warner said, "is actually only twenty and I am by law her Guardian until she is twenty-one. She will therefore return home with me and give up this ridiculous charade."

"I am afraid that is impossible."

"What do you mean by impossible? As I have just told you, my Lord, she has to obey me until she is of age."

"That is where your information about this young lady is at fault," the Marquis responded.

"I just cannot think why you should say that," Cyril Warner said. "I intend to assert myself as I am entitled to do and she will pack and leave with me immediately."

Eleta felt a quiver go through Pepe.

She pulled the child closer to her and at the same time in case she should speak she put her finger on her lips.

"Then I am afraid, Mr. Warner, that you will be disappointed," the Marquis said, "when I tell you that your stepdaughter is in fact my wife."

"*Your wife*! I don't believe it. If it had been in the newspapers, I would have been aware of it."

"I agree and so would the rest of the world. But unfortunately, as one of my relatives has just died, I am in deep mourning. I am therefore waiting for the funeral to be over before the announcement of our wedding is sent to *The Gazette*."

"I can hardly believe your Lordship has married a woman you thought to be a Governess," he snarled angrily.

"That is my business," the Marquis replied, "and, as there is no more to say on the subject, I can only tell you that your visit here is fruitless. You will be informed the day before our wedding is formally announced."

As he spoke, he put out his hand towards the bell-pull on the wall beside him.

Almost immediately the door opened and Harris appeared.

"Will you show Mr. Warner to his carriage," the Marquis ordered.

For a moment Cyril Warner hesitated and there was no doubt the fury expressed in his face was about to pour out through his lips.

The Marquis walked away towards the window and stood looking out at the garden with his back to him.

Harris now had the door wide open and there was nothing Cyril Warner could do but leave.

He walked out muttering beneath his breath.

Then, as the door closed, Pepe jumped up and ran towards her father.

"You saved her! You saved her, Daddy," she cried. "Oh, you are clever, so very clever."

"Go and see that that dreadful man drives away," the Marquis said, "and I don't want him to talk to or ask questions of Harris or the footmen."

Pepe understood and ran across the room.

Eleta stood looking at the Marquis.

"That was a very astute way of getting rid of him, my Lord, but I am afraid that he will eventually find out the truth."

The Marquis smiled.

"If it is not before midnight tonight, he will be *too late!*"

Eleta looked at him, not understanding what he was saying.

He put his arms round her.

"I have loved you ever since I first saw you," he said. "I was just waiting for an opportunity to tell you so."

Before she could realise what was happening, his lips were on hers.

He kissed her at first very gently.

Then, as if he was unable to control the excitement within him, more ardently and more passionately.

She felt herself quiver with a wild thrill that was so completely different from anything she had ever known.

Then, as the Marquis raised his head, she said in a voice he could hardly hear,

"This cannot be true."

"It is true, my darling one. I love you and I think, because I see it in your eyes, that you love me a little."

"I love you more than I can possibly say," Eleta breathed, "but how could you ask me to marry you when you don't even know my real name?"

"Does it matter?" he asked. "What matters is that we have found each other. I have been looking for you all my life and, as you have travelled to a lot of strange places and not found a husband, I think that you were looking for me."

"Of course I was looking for you, but I thought you were only in my dreams," Eleta whispered.

"That is where I intend always to be. So we will be married this evening and I am going to send now for the Vicar who is also my private Chaplain. As you know, I do not need to have a Marriage Licence because my Chapel, although consecrated, is private."

"How can this be true," Eleta asked, "when I have been so frightened that I would have to marry that dreadful Duke?"

"Duke?" the Marquis questioned.

Eleta laughed.

"I have only just remembered you don't know my name!"

"I cannot really believe that you are related to that ghastly man who has just left – "

"He only married my Mama after my father died."

"And who was your father?"

"He was the Earl of Stanrenton," Eleta replied.

The Marquis stared at her and then he laughed.

"I don't believe it! My relations have been telling me for a long time I should marry 'someone suitable'. Of course what they really meant was the daughter of a Peer, and that, without any prompting from them, is exactly what I have done. I remember your father's name because my father knew him well."

"I was very young when my father died, so I have never known much about his friends. My mother was a wonderful person, but very lonely after my father's death. That is why she married that horrible Cyril Warner."

"I thought he was extremely unpleasant, especially the way he talked about you."

"He wanted the Duke of Hazelware, who is well over fifty, to marry me and then be Chairman of one of his businesses. He is a ship-builder."

"Well, as far as I am concerned," the Marquis said, "he can take his ships to 'Nowhere Land' and stay there. All I want, my darling, is that you and I should be married at once and the one person who will be most delighted is of course Pepe. She will have the mother she has never had."

"I love Pepe," Eleta sighed.

She moved closer to him before she whispered,

"Of course I know that you want a son and I hope I can give you a lot of sons as handsome and as marvellous as you."

The Marquis could not find words to answer.

He just kissed her.

He kissed her until Eleta thought that they were no longer two people but one.

*

When Pepe returned a little later, they were sitting on the sofa holding hands.

She burst into the room saying,

"He has gone! He has gone! He tried to talk to Harris, but he saw me listening and went outside. Then, when he turned back, I glared at him from the top of the steps. So he got into his carriage and drove away!"

"I hope he went down the drive without stopping."

"I watched until he drove out through the gates and now he has gone, Miss Lawson can stay with us!"

"She is staying with us for ever," the Marquis said.

Pepe gave a leap of joy.

"For ever and ever. In fact the only way I can keep her is by marrying her immediately before Cyril Warner finds out that I was telling a lie!"

"Please can I come to the wedding?" Pepe asked.

"But, of course, and you will be the most important person there. And, as we are to be married this evening, I think you ought to rest this afternoon, otherwise you will fall asleep in the Chapel."

"I will not do that because I will be too excited," Pepe enthused. "Oh, it's wonderful, wonderful – "

Then she stopped.

"If you are my Daddy and you marry Miss Lawson, then she will be my Mummy. And I have always wanted a Mummy."

"Of course I will be your Mummy, even though I will be a Step-Mummy," Eleta said. "But we will all be very happy, I promise you."

"Very very happy," Pepe sighed, "and even though you love Daddy, you will still love me too."

"You have a very special part of my heart and your father has another special part, so it is quite fair."

"I will do the same with my heart, half for you and half for Daddy!"

"If you add it up," the Marquis said, "it only makes one complete heart and that is what will make this house a very special home and a very special happy place."

Pepe put her arms round his neck and kissed him.

"Thank you, thank you, Daddy, for saving Eleta, as I now can call her, and keeping her here with us for ever."

"For ever and ever," the Marquis sighed.

As the Marquis kissed Eleta again, the door opened and Harris spoke up,

"There's someone to see Miss Lawson, who says she's come all the way from London."

To the Marquis's surprise, Eleta exclaimed,

"From London? I know who she is. Bring her in, I want her Ladyship to meet her."

"Very good, miss."

As he left the room, the Marquis looked at Eleta questioningly.

"Who is this?"

"She is someone very important who I want here, especially after what you have just said."

The Marquis did not understand.

But before he could say anything, Bates announced,

"Miss Betty Ludlow."

As she came into the room, Eleta jumped up and ran towards her and threw her arms round her.

"Betty, dearest," she cried. "I am so glad to see you. In fact I was just going to get in touch with you."

"I came to warn you," Betty said, "that the Master's found out where you are, but, as I passed by his carriage comin' through the village, I knew I were too late."

"You are not too late for me, Betty, I want you to meet the Marquis."

She turned towards him to say,

"Betty was my mother's lady's-maid and, since her death, she has looked after me. And she is the kindest and dearest person I know."

She smiled before she added,

"It was her idea that I should go to the Agency and find somewhere to hide. That is how I came here in the first place."

"I am very delighted to meet you," the Marquis said holding out his hand to Betty, "and I can only thank you from the bottom of my heart, because she has altered our whole lives and made us happier than I could possibly tell you in words."

"So your stepfather has gone away?" Betty asked. "I could hardly believe my eyes when I saw him leavin' alone. I thought you would have had to be with him."

"I would have been," Eleta said, "but I am going to be married this evening to his Lordship."

Betty clasped her hands together.

"So you have found someone to love! It's what I prayed and prayed you would find and it makes me happier than I can possibly say."

"And I am indeed the luckiest man in the world," the Marquis said. "So I hope Betty, if my wife wants you, you will stay here with her."

"Of course I will," Betty answered.

"I have been thinking, Eleta said, "that if we do have a short honeymoon, Betty will look after Pepe for us. She knows marvellous stories, even better than the ones I have told Pepe."

"I wouldn't say that," Betty replied, "but I knows some stories this young lady would enjoy."

"I love stories," Pepe exclaimed.

She had obviously taken to Betty, Eleta thought, because she was looking up at her with wide eyes.

"Well, I am thankful you are here, Betty, and of course Pepe will show you where we are sleeping and I am certain you can have a room near us."

She glanced at the Marquis as she spoke in case he objected, but he merely remarked,

"If Betty is kind enough to help you look after Pepe that will give me a little more time to be with you."

"I knew you would understand."

*

154

That night after Eleta and the Marquis had been married in the Chapel with Betty and Pepe as witnesses, the whole household drank their health in champagne.

Monsieur Téyson promised them a proper wedding cake the next day, but, at a moment's notice, he produced one made of ice-cream with a candle on top of it and with a mass of *petits fours* round it to please Pepe.

It was certainly, Eleta thought, happier than any wedding celebration she had ever attended.

*

When Pepe had been put to bed, she lay in the big canopied bed waiting for the Marquis.

Her prayers had been answered.

She could hardly believe it possible that she could be so deliriously happy.

The Marquis came in and, taking off the dark robe he was wearing, climbed into the bed.

He took her in his arms.

"Is this really happening to us?" he asked. "I just cannot help thinking that I will wake up and find it is all a dream or part of my imagination."

"I only know I love you," Eleta answered, "and everything that has happened to us seems as if one of the stars has fallen down from the sky."

"That is what I am feeling too," he said. "You are so beautiful in every way and I knew the moment I saw you that I wanted you to be mine. But I thought it was one of those ambitions that would never come true."

"And now it has," Eleta whispered.

"And I have no words to express the way I am now feeling," the Marquis sighed.

Then he was kissing her, kissing her so that once again he was taking her up into the sky.

He kissed her until they were quivering with the wonder of their ecstasy.

Then, as the Marquis made her his, they touched the Heaven which all people seek but few are fortunate enough to find.

It is the Heaven that God keeps especially for lovers.

The love they give each other that comes from God, belongs to God and is theirs for Eternity.